JADED

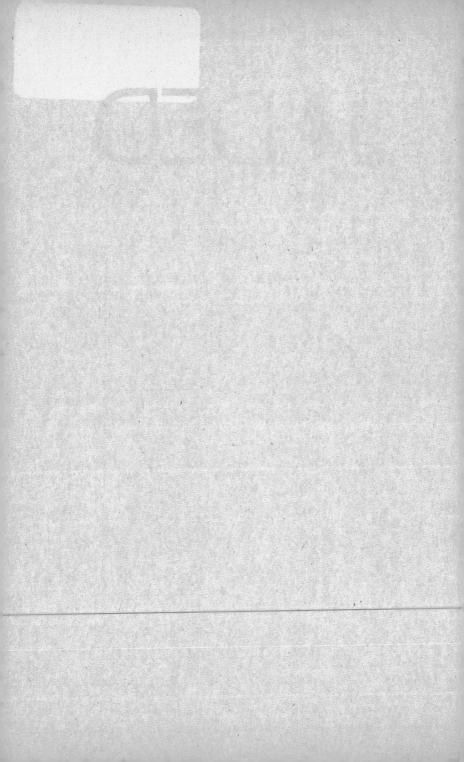

JADED

Monica McKayhan

JADED

ISBN-13: 978-0-373-83099-2
ISBN-10: 0-373-83099-8

www.KimaniTRU.com

Printed in U.S.A.

Acknowledgments

God is the source of my talent and blessings.

To my husband, Mark, who is my inspiration.

I'd like to give a special shout-out to a few young people: my sons Brandon, Erik, Mark Jr., Keimar and DeAndre. I love you, Ricky, DJ and Devric—forever and always! Thanks to my daughter, Damarka, and my niece, Keya McGathy, for your love and support. My parents, Johnetta and Tyree Davis, are two of my greatest supporters. And the young people everywhere who have read and loved *Indigo Summer*...keep reading.

For those young people out there who are just like Terrence, having to become a man too soon—and not being able to just be a teenager—keep your head up! The things we endure in life build great character.

one

Jade

I sat on top of a cardboard box—a box filled with all of the colorful sweaters my mother had bought for me over the years. There was the red turtleneck, and the brown one with the fuzz balls all over it and the yellow one that tied around the waist—the yellow one looked like one my grandmother would wear to church. I had refused to wear any of them, and some of them even had the tags still on them. My mother wasn't the best at picking out clothes for me, and I just wished she'd stop trying. It would save us both a lot of time and trouble.

She insisted that she knew my style, but the reality was she really didn't. She knew her own style that she wanted to be mine. And our tastes couldn't have been more different. If she knew my style, she would've stocked my closet with blue jeans that were tight in the hips and narrow at the ankles—the kind I would wear with the wedge-heeled sandals that I'd picked up at Bakers shoe store over the summer. Or she'd pick out one of those cute little cropped tops that you could only find at Charlotte Russe or the Papaya stores at the mall. She might even take the liberty of popping her head inside Forever 21 and sorting through the clearance rack for that one-of-a-kind sweater that I would actually wear. But she didn't even know that those stores existed. She had tunnel vision when she visited the mall. The only stores she recognized were JCPenney and Macy's because she carried around their charge cards in her purse. I don't know why she carried them, because most of the time they were maxed out.

She didn't know me at all. Because if she did, she'd realize how unhappy I was with this new living arrangement that she'd come up with. A three-bedroom apartment in the same apartment complex that my father lived in. He lived in Building 300 near the playground, and we lived in the new section of the complex—in Building 700 near the pool. My bedroom window faced the back side of the complex, and the only view I had was of the highway where millions of cars traveled each day. I couldn't even see the front of the building where the kids my age hung out. At least at my father's apartment, I could see who was outside—and could decide if I wanted to go outside or not.

Sometimes Felicia Clark and Angie Miller would be outside talking trash to some girls from another neighborhood, or some boys from school would be in the parking lot leaned against their cars with their music blasting. At Daddy's I could see the pool and knew who was going for a swim. And at least in my old bedroom I could watch Chocolate Boy pull up on his little brother's bike when he snuck over for a visit. I could see him riding up the hill, breathing hard as he got closer. He would lift the bike onto his shoulder and carry it up the flight of stairs and to my front door. Mrs. Hernandez on the second floor would always frown as he took the stairs two at a time. She was so nosy—I couldn't stand her. I was sure that she'd stop my father on his way home from work one day and tell him that Chocolate Boy had spent the day at our house—even though he wasn't allowed to visit unless Daddy was home. What Daddy didn't know didn't hurt him, though. But if he ever found out, I would blame Mrs. Hernandez.

It was easy having a life while living with Daddy, because he was never there. He was always working late at the office, or hanging out with his new girlfriend Veronica. Veronica was a home wrecker in my opinion—if I was allowed to have an opinion, but most of the time nobody asked for it. My parents were divorced, but on the verge of getting back together. At least I thought they were—until now. Now I wasn't sure what they were doing. This was not my idea of bringing my family back together—living in separate apartments. We were supposed to be living together. Instead it seemed that we were moving further apart, and no one seemed to see it but me. I still couldn't understand why we couldn't have just moved in with Daddy, he and Mommy work out their differences and we become one big, happy family again. I guess that was too much to ask God for, because after all the praying I had done, he still didn't see fit to grant me that one thing. Even after I told him how good I would behave, and not get into any trouble in the upcoming school year. I even promised to keep my room and the kitchen clean before being asked. I guess he didn't believe me. I guess my track record with him wasn't that great, after all. After all, I hadn't been to church on Sunday in I don't know how long, even though that was the last promise I'd made.

I had been tricked into thinking that my family was on the road to getting back together. When my parents got a divorce during the summer before my freshman year, I thought my world had come to an end. Mommy took Mattie and me and headed for New Jersey to live with my grandmother. I was miserable the moment I set foot in Grandmother's house—a house that smelled of mothballs and milk of magnesia—and she started setting rules that were almost impossible to follow. Mattie and I couldn't even walk across the shiny hardwood floors in the dining room without being accused of walking too loud. Or if I played my CDs at all, she'd yell at me to turn the music down.

"It's the devil's music," she'd say. And I'd roll my eyes and turn it down.

I would pray that we would get out of her house soon. She forced us to go to church several times a week, and would quiz us about what the preacher had talked about. I failed every one of those quizzes, because most of the time I'd fallen asleep right there on the back pew—my mouth open wide, sometimes with drool creeping down the side of my face. But I didn't care. There was nothing exciting about listening to someone say the same scripture over and over again, and beat it in the ground. Grandmother's church was nothing like our church in Atlanta, where we had a youth ministry that was actually interesting. We discussed things that pertained to kids my age, like boys, sex and school. We could discuss our thoughts about things and not be ashamed of what we said. I was starting to miss Atlanta more and more each day.

By the middle of my freshman year, I'd already decided that Grandmother's house was no place for me, and that I needed to be back in A-T-L. But not only that, I needed to reunite my family. My parents still loved each other—they had to. And it was my goal to find out just how much. When I got into trouble at school, it forced my mother to ship me back to Atlanta to live with my father for a little while. My plan seemed to be heading in the right direction at that point. That is until I ran into the infamous Mr. Collins, my American history teacher, who thought that it was okay to touch me in an inappropriate way. It was the most humiliating experience of my life. As soon as my mother found out, she hopped a flight back to Atlanta just to make sure he was not only fired from my high school, but that he was also arrested and thrown behind bars. Mommy was so brave and didn't even flinch when Mr. Collins walked past, his arms in handcuffs, giving us the evil eye as two police officers escorted him off campus. She gave him the evil eye right back. I felt so protected and secure, and felt that there was nothing my mother couldn't handle. As different as we were, Mommy and I, at that moment I wanted to be just like her—brave and strong.

I still remember the excitement I felt when Mommy and Mattie had shown up at the Hartsfield-Jackson Atlanta Airport and the four of us ended up at Red Lobster for dinner. I knew it was just a matter of time before our family would be back together. And when I caught my parents kissing each other—on the lips—in the middle of my daddy's kitchen, and holding each other like they used to, I knew that they belonged together.

"So when are you and Daddy getting remarried?" I asked Mommy one morning when she was flipping pancakes and wearing one of Daddy's Falcons' jerseys.

"We hadn't really talked about that, Jade-bug," she said, and squeezed my nose like she used to when I was a little girl. "I'm not even sure that's what we both want."

"What do you mean you're not sure? Don't you still love each other?"

"Of course we do, baby. I will always love your father, and he will always love me. After all, we gave each other two beautiful girls, you and Mattie. But that doesn't mean that we should be remarried."

"I don't get it," I said, holding on to the bottle of Mrs. Butterworth's maple syrup.

"What don't you get, Jade?" Mommy asked and stacked three pancakes onto Mattie's plate.

"I don't get why we're here...together...in Daddy's apartment. The two of you are running around here kissing each other like you're still in love. Look at you...you're wearing his jersey and sleeping in the same room with him!" I felt like tears might start falling if I said any more, so I shut up.

"Jade, your father and I have apologized to each other for hurting one another. We have made amends, and now we're just enjoying each other's company. We're better friends now, and we both agree that we enjoy our freedom."

"Are you and Mattie moving back to Atlanta?" I asked and set the bottle of syrup in front of Mattie, and then placed my hands on my hips, the legs of my pajama pants touching the floor. I waited for an answer.

"I'm thinking about moving back," she said. "I know it's hard living with Grandmother. And I know that you and Mattie want to be near your father. It feels like the right thing to do."

"So we're moving in with Daddy?" Mattie asked, her mouth filled with pancakes.

"Don't talk with your mouth full, little girl," Mommy told her and then handed her a paper towel to wipe her mouth with. "We're moving back to Atlanta, but I don't think we're going to be moving in with Daddy."

"You're kidding, right?" I asked, not believing my ears.

"No, I'm not kidding," Mommy said. "In fact, I looked at an apartment yesterday and put a deposit down on it."

"An apartment where?" I asked.

"Right here in this complex," she said in a matter-of-fact sort of way. "That way you can continue to go to the same school, and Mattie can go to her old elementary school."

She didn't seem to be bothered by the fact that we'd be wasting a whole lot of money by spending it on separate apartments, when Daddy had plenty of room right here for all of us. And what was worse was that we'd be wasting money on an apartment in the same complex. Parents were strange. She was always telling me to think things through, and here she was not thinking at all.

"How many pancakes you want, Jade-bug?" she asked, changing the subject.

Suddenly my appetite was gone, and I wanted nothing more than to rush to my room and cover my head with a pillow.

"Not hungry," I mumbled and walked out of the kitchen. Left her standing there with a spatula in her hand and that Aunt Jemima-looking scarf on her head.

I made my way down the hallway to my room, my head hung low as I looked down at my big fuzzy pink slippers the whole way. Once in my room, I bounced onto the bed, covered my ears with the earphones of my iPod. Keyshia

Cole was spilling her lyrics into my ears. I normally liked Keyshia Cole, but for some reason she sounded whiny at the moment. So I pressed the stop button and threw my iPod aside. I picked up my cell phone to see if I had any missed calls. There weren't any missed calls, but I had a text message.

"What u doin?" Chocolate Boy asked.

Chocolate Boy. The newfound love of my life, also known as Terrence. He was my first and only real boyfriend. A boy who had sat next to me in Mr. Collins's American history class, and slipped me notes from across the room. When he asked me to be his girl, I thought he was joking. But he showed me just how serious he was when he gave me a heart-shaped locket with his picture stuck all in it. I wore it every single day. We had become inseparable over the summer, and were already talking about sharing a locker in the upcoming school year. Things were getting pretty serious.

"Arguing w/M." I sent a text back.

"Again?" he asked.

"Yes."

"Not da end of the world, Morgan."

He always called me by my last name—Morgan, as if we were in boot camp or something.

"U always take her side."

"I'm on your side..."

I disagreed, and was done texting with him. I shut my pink Razor phone, and threw it against the pillow, turned on my clock radio and tuned it to 107.9, Atlanta's hip-hop station, shut my eyes and enjoyed the music.

That was three weeks ago, and now as I sat staring out of my new bedroom window, tears began to fill my eyes. The rain bounced against the window and played a tune on the pane. It sounded like somebody was playing the drums. I glanced across the room at my bed frame and mattress that leaned against the wall—still needing to be put together. Daddy had called earlier and was supposed to be on his way to put beds and tables together, but so far, he hadn't shown up. I could hear Mommy and Mattie in the living room, unpacking boxes and singing some Marvin Gaye song at the top of their lungs. They acted as if this was a happy occasion. How could they be dancing and singing during a time such as this—when our lives were falling apart?

two

Terrence

I hadn't quite learned how to do cornrows, but I had mastered a basic ponytail and could snap a barrette better than your average woman. If Sydney wasn't so tender-headed, and would sit still, her braids might actually go in the right direction. But instead, she was always squirming and as a result, one braid was sticking straight up, while the other one was at a right angle. She didn't care. She was so busy trying to get outside to ride her bike with Cee Cee, the little girl down the block, that she didn't mind if her hair was all over her head.

Cee Cee got a shiny new red bike for Christmas, the kind with colorful plastic streamers hanging from the handlebars, and red and yellow reflectors on the wheels. She also had a silver horn that she blew like she was crazy, while riding up and down the block. Sydney's bike wasn't quite as flashy. Hers was originally an old dirt bike that one of our neighbors had placed at the curb on trash day. I spotted it, picked it up and took it to our garage, patched up the flat tire, painted it pink—Sydney's favorite color—and placed a few UNO cards between the spokes in the wheels to take the place of reflectors. She complained daily that her bike wasn't as cool as Cee Cee's, but I reminded her of the fact that several kids in our neighborhood weren't fortunate enough to have a bike at all. And that she should be grateful for what she had.

We were all fortunate for what we had—which wasn't much. Just a run-down two-bedroom house, where the lights barely stayed on and the water was off more often than it was on. Groceries were hard to come by, too, and oftentimes we went without eating. Most of the time I doubled up on lunch, because we received free lunch, and bypassed dinner altogether. I encouraged my younger sister and brother to do the same, but most of the time they still complained about being hungry. It was those times that I was forced to splurge on a cheese pizza or a box of chicken, but only on the days that they were running a special. Times were hard, and the paycheck I received from working part-time and weekends at Big Tony's Automotive Shop was barely enough to cover the bills and food.

Sometimes Tony paid me for hours that I hadn't even worked, especially after he discovered that I was taking care of my younger brother and sister. He didn't treat me with pity, but instead commended me for being a man.

"You just like me, boy," he said one day, his size-thirteen boots propped up on his desk, oil all over his hands as he wiped them clean with an old rag. "I had to take care of my little brother when my mother passed away. It takes a real man to fill them shoes. And I'm proud of you, son."

That meant a lot coming from Big Tony, especially since he was somebody that I looked up to. He had owned his own repair shop since he was seventeen. He drove a pimped-out Cadillac, and he tinkered with the engine on a daily basis. Big Tony wore an old-school afro, and a beard that was in desperate need of a trim. His stomach hung over the front of his belt, and when he talked he sounded just like Barry White with a Southern accent. His Mississippi roots almost made him seem country, but he was cool with me. I was grateful to him for giving me a job when I was only twelve years old. And it only took me two years to be promoted from the guy who pulled the cars into the garage to be repaired, to the guy who fixed brakes, performed oil changes and replaced old spark plugs with new ones. One time Big Tony even let me help him change an alternator.

Big Tony used to be a professional wrestler back in his younger days, placing his opponents in headlocks and choke holds. He was known for his outrageous power slams. I tried to imagine his 250-pound frame slamming down onto someone's ribs at full force, and all I could think of was pain. And when he told his stories of his wrestling days, he talked about how he dominated the industry. He was much bigger than 250, he claimed.

"I was more like 350, Youngblood," he'd say, "but I was quick!"

Youngblood was a nickname that he'd given me. He said that I was still wet behind the ears and still had milk in the corners of my mouth, which meant that I was still a youngster.

"You don't know nothing about life," he'd say, "just live a little longer."

I loved talking to Big Tony about things like girls, school and life in general—he was wise. He talked a lot about his younger days, and his wrestling career. He even told me about his ex-wife, Norma, the one who ran off with his kids and didn't leave a number or forwarding address where he could contact them. And now that his kids were grown and had families of their own, they didn't want to have anything to do with him. They blamed him for their mother leaving. And because she never gave them the cards and letters he wrote, they thought he had abandoned them. He didn't have a good relationship with them, not like he wanted to. He wished that he could see his grandchildren, but his son and daughter wouldn't allow that. Last Christmas he spent the entire day putting a new motor into Mr. Henderson's Ford F150, because he didn't have a family to spend the holidays with. It was the saddest thing I'd ever seen.

At least I had Sydney and Trey, my younger sister and

brother. Sydney had been a tomboy since she was two years old, trying her best to keep up with me. Even at eleven years old, she still preferred to shoot hoops with the boys in our neighborhood rather than play with Barbies. Occasionally she would ride her bike with Cee Cee or spend hours at her friend Alexis's house wearing out her Playstation—and even then she preferred Madden or NBA Live. I swore that this upcoming Christmas I would buy her a Playstation of her own, and if I was lucky, I'd get her the new NBA game to go with it. That's if I was lucky.

Trey was into music. He knew his way around a keyboard better than any adult that I'd ever met. At eight years old, Trey made beats for all the teenage boys in our neighborhood that they would then compose raps and lyrics to. People were constantly knocking on our door at odd hours, looking for Trey and his beats. He could probably make a whole lot of money if he actually charged for his music, but I didn't want to complicate his young life. Besides, most of the guys he made beats for were our friends—my friends, anyway—the ones I'd grown up with since kindergarten. How would you put a price on friendship? And besides, I lost count of the number of meals we'd eaten at their houses, or the number of nights we slept over because we didn't have lights or gas at our house in the wintertime.

I'd become the man of the house three years ago, when Arlene just up and went away and didn't come back for several months. Arlene—that's my mom. She told us not to call her Mom because she wasn't that old. At the tender age of thirty-two, she felt like she was too young to have a sixteen-year-old son. But when you get pregnant when you're sixteen, that's what happens—your life moves too fast, and your kids grow up faster than you expect them to. You add drugs to that equation, and your life moves faster than an Amtrak train on a tight schedule. That's what happened to Arlene—she found drugs and her life moved way too fast. It moved so fast that she forgot she had three kids to take care of.

The first time she left was the day before my thirteenth birthday. I remember it so well. It was a Friday night and she kept telling me the whole week before that we were going to Dave & Buster's on Saturday for my birthday, and that I could play as many games as I wanted to play. She said that we would order pizza, and drink as many Cokes as our stomachs would hold. She even said that I could invite Damian and Julius, my two best friends who lived just a block away. We had already talked about the games we intended to play and I had already bragged about how I was going to whip them at every game in the place.

When Aunt Brenda pulled up to the curb in her boyfriend's Caprice Classic, with rust on the side and the velvet seats that had cigarette burns all over them, I knew that the plans had changed. She staggered into our kitchen, wearing a short miniskirt, a tube top and too much makeup on her face. She was holding on to a Miller beer in one hand and a lit Newport cigarette in her other hand, and telling Arlene to hurry up.

"Where y'all going, Aunt Brenda?" I asked, a bowl of Froot Loops in my hand. It was all we had to eat in the house that day.

"We going out to the club, boy, you know…shake our booties!" Aunt Brenda said and started swaying her hips to her own music, and then planted a kiss on my forehead. She smelled like beer and old perfume all mixed together. "I heard you got a birthday tomorrow. Is that true, boy?"

"Yep!" I said.

"How old you gon' be?" she asked.

"Thirteen."

"Ooh, you almost a man now," she teased and smiled.

Aunt Brenda wasn't our real aunt. She had just been my mother's best friend for as long as I could remember, and she made us call her Aunt Brenda. "Put a handle on my name," she would always say. Miss Brenda sounded so formal, so Aunt Brenda seemed like the perfect name for her.

"He ain't no man yet," Arlene said as she walked into the room, dressed like Aunt Brenda in a similar miniskirt, and a top that showed too much skin, in my opinion. She grabbed Aunt Brenda's cigarette right out of her hand and took a puff.

"Are you gonna be home in time to take me to Dave & Buster's tomorrow?" I asked Arlene.

"Of course I'll be home, Tee," she said. "Didn't I tell you that we were going?"

"Yes, ma'am."

"Can I go, Mommy?" Sydney asked.

"I don't know, baby, you'll have to ask Tee. He might not want no little raggedy girls hanging around with him and his friends," she said. "And what I tell you about calling me Mommy? My name is Arlene. I'm too young to be referred to as anybody's mama!" She struck a pose with her hands on her hips, as if to prove that she was still young and beautiful. She kissed Sydney on the cheek and then wiped away the lipstick she left behind. She kissed my cheek and did the same thing. "Where's my baby?"

"He's in there watching *Dragon Ball Z,*" Sydney said.

"Trey!" Arlene called to him and he came running into the kitchen. "Come and give me some sugar, boy."

Trey rushed into the kitchen and slammed into my mother, hugged her tightly around the waist and then she kissed him on the cheek.

"You be a good boy until I get back, okay? Do what your big brother tells you."

"Yes, ma'am," Trey said.

"Tee, I want you to get this kitchen cleaned up. And, Sydney, you help. I don't wanna see these dirty dishes in the sink when I get back."

"Okay," I said and slurped the rest of my milk down.

"There's nothing to eat here, Mommy…I mean Arlene. Nothing except cereal, and I'm tired of eating Froot Loops," Sydney whined.

"Well, unless you have some money to buy something

else, I guess you'll be eating what's here," Arlene declared and placed her hands on her hips and shook her neck from side to side.

Aunt Brenda reached down into her glittery purse and pulled out a ten-dollar bill.

"Here, y'all run on down the street and grab a box of chicken," she ordered and snatched her cigarette back from Arlene, took a puff. "Come on, girl, let's go."

I watched out of the kitchen window as the Caprice Classic pulled away from the curb, sounding as if it needed a new muffler and looking like it needed a paint job. I wondered what adventure awaited them in the streets of Atlanta that night. It seemed that every weekend it was a new one. But more important, I wondered what time they were coming back, and if I would make it to Dave & Buster's at all. Not only didn't she come home that night—she didn't come home for a whole week.

I was used to waking up Sydney and Trey in the mornings and making sure they got to school, but trying to figure out what to eat—well, that brought about a new challenge. Arlene had left us with an almost empty refrigerator, with nothing more than a gallon of milk and two leftover pork chops from last Sunday's dinner. There was half a box of Froot Loops on top of the refrigerator, and a can of green beans on the shelf. By the middle of the week, I received a fifty-dollar paycheck from working at Big Tony's. It wasn't much, but it was all we had under the circumstances. I cashed it, and the three of us loaded into the backseat of a yellow cab which drove us a couple of blocks to the supermarket. We rushed into Publix and loaded our shopping cart with hot dogs, potato chips, soda pop and Twinkies—enough to tide us over until Arlene decided to come back home. My paycheck wasn't much, but at least it fed us for a few days.

By the time she walked through the door, I had long forgotten about my birthday and Dave & Buster's. I was just happy to see her. I wrapped my arms around her waist and hugged her, despite the way she smelled. She was still wearing the same clothes she'd left home in five days before. She seemed oblivious to anything around her, and stumbled into her bedroom. She climbed into bed fully clothed, and I just stood in the doorway watching as she drifted into a heavy sleep. I pulled her shoes from her worn feet and grabbed the quilt from the foot of her bed, placed it over her body and then kissed her cheek. Before I left the room she was already snoring.

That week changed me, I thought, as I placed a pink barrette on the end of Sydney's ponytail. I watched as she hopped onto her bike that I'd fixed up and painted pink for her. I knew that I'd become a man long before the average boy did.

three

Jade

The first day of school and Chocolate Boy was leaning against my locker, wearing a beautiful smile, a pair of sagging jeans and holding a pretty little yellow flower in his hand.

"What took you so long?" he asked and grinned.

"I missed the bus, and my mother had to bring me," I groaned. "I couldn't find the black jeans I wanted to wear. Since we moved, I haven't been able to find anything! It's chaos at my house."

"I like the jeans you have on," he said, referring to the blue ones that I decided on instead. "This is for you."

"Thank you," I said and smiled and took the flower from his hand.

"Where's your first class?"

"Second floor, Miss Reynolds," I told him. "But I gotta go find Indigo. She was supposed to meet me here."

Indigo Summer looked radiant in her skinny black jeans, and a sexy fuchsia baby-doll top with rhinestones around the neck. She wore fuchsia sandals to match. She looked as if she'd been in the sun, and had picked up a few extra pounds over the summer. This was the first summer that we hadn't spent together. Instead, she went to Chicago to see her grandmother, and ended up doing some wild and crazy things with her cousin, Sabrina. Sabrina had her shaking her booty at an adult nightclub, among other things that we hadn't discussed yet. We would definitely have to get caught up on all the gossip before the week was over.

She screamed when she spotted me.

"Jade!" We hugged each other. I checked out her hair, and she checked out mine. "You got your hair cut," she said and smiled. "That's hot!"

"Those jeans are cute, too, girl," I told her. "You get 'em at 5-7-9?"

"Charlotte Russe," she said and struck a pose, "after clearance sale."

"And the top?"

"Papaya."

I guess Chocolate Boy wasn't feeling our girlie conversation and became restless.

"Hey, what's up, Indi?" he asked.

"Hey, Terrence."

"I'ma check you later, Morgan," he said, his algebra book under his arm. "You got dance team practice after school?"

"Yes."

"Cool, I'll meet you here and walk you down to the gym."

"Cool," I said and smiled as Chocolate Boy strolled down the hallway in his baggy jeans.

"You and him seem pretty close all of a sudden. What's up with that?"

"We been hanging out," I said, and grabbed my three-ring binder out of my locker. "We're thinking about sharing a locker."

"Oh, now that's serious," she said and laughed. "Have you thought about doing a prenup, too?"

"Shut up, girl," I teased and laughed as I slammed my locker shut and headed down the hallway. "I can't wait to get to practice this afternoon. Freshmen tryouts are today."

"Yep, I remember those from last year. Tryouts were pretty intense," Indigo said. "It's nice to be returning sophomores and not having to try out again. That was so frustrating! Wondering if I would make the team or not. And then my dance partner and best friend moved away right in the middle of all of it."

"I'm sorry," I told her. I was the dance partner and best friend she was referring to. When my parents got a divorce, it changed everything—all of our plans. "How was I supposed to know that we were moving to New Jersey?"

"You got lucky, moving back to Atlanta and being able to snatch a spot on the dance team in the middle of the year like that."

"It wasn't luck, boo. It was fate," I said and snapped my fingers in front of Indigo. "Some things are just meant to be."

"I know some girls who wanted to beat your behind. Some girls who had gone through tryouts at the beginning of the year, and didn't make the team."

"There was a reason they didn't make the team. And it wasn't because of me," I boasted. "Miss Martin knew I had talent. Me and you could dance rings around all of those girls out there."

"What's up, hoochie?" Tameka, one of the girls on the dance team, walked up and said.

She and Indigo started screaming and hugging each other, acting as if they'd lost their minds.

"What's up, Tameka?" I asked.

"Nothing much," she said and then dismissed me. "Indi, you and Marcus going to the homecoming dance?"

"Probably so," Indigo said. "What about you?"

"Of course. I wouldn't miss it for the world," she said. "You wanna go dress shopping this weekend?"

"You know I do," Indigo said.

"Well, ask your mama if you can spend the weekend," she said. "My mama has been asking about you, anyway."

"That sounds good," Indigo said. "How about Jade? Can she come, too?"

Tameka thought for a moment, glanced my way as if Indi had caught her off guard. She looked me up and down and then put a fake smile on her face. "She can come if she wants to."

"Of course she wants to," Indigo said before I could respond. "We'll be there."

"Okay, I'll see you later, hoochie, at dance team practice."

In an instant she was gone, and I was glad. I immediately started thinking of an excuse to get out of going to Tameka's house. How dare Indigo Summer plan my weekend for me like that? Who did she think she was, anyway? Tameka wasn't my favorite person in the world. After all, she almost stole my best friend away after I moved to New Jersey. Every time I talked to Indigo on the phone, she was going shopping with Tameka, or to the movies with Tameka, or just hanging out at Applebee's...*with Tameka.* Tameka this...Tameka that. I got sick of hearing her name.

"I don't appreciate you planning my weekend for me, *hoochie,*" I said and sarcastically used Tameka's pet name.

"Oh, please...you don't have anything else to do...except stand around in the parking lot of your apartment complex, gossiping with Felicia and Angie. That's such a waste of time," she said. "And you can't stand your home life, right?"

She was right about that. I hated my home life.

"Besides, it'll be fun hanging out at Tameka's. Mel, her mom, is crazy cool. You will love her," she said and then headed toward her English class. "Ask your mom if it's okay."

Before I could respond, Indigo had disappeared into a

crowd of people, leaving me in the middle of the hallway. Secretly I was excited about the prospect of spending the weekend at Tameka's house. It was a change—something to do, other than sit around and be bored at home. Chocolate Boy usually worked on the weekends, so the chances of us hanging out were slim to none. Not to mention, he spent a lot of time with his younger sister and brother. When we talked on the phone, I always heard them in the background fighting or asking him what was for dinner. I guessed that his mother worked a lot, too, because she was never there.

Dance team tryouts were the best way of finding out which girls were considered to be the cream of the crop, and which girls weren't. Indigo, Tameka and I sat in the bleachers and watched the freshmen girls shake their booties to music that they'd chosen for their routines. We picked out the girls that we thought would make the team, and dismissed the ones we thought should've stayed at home. Some of the routines were whack, but some of the girls, we knew, were a sure shot. They had natural rhythm, some of them, and Miss Martin would be crazy not to select them for the team.

Toward the end of tryouts, some of the football players breezed into the gymnasium, Quincy Rawlins leading the pack, along with Jason Russell, Paul Bell and some of the new freshmen players that I didn't recognize. They couldn't wait to stop by and check out the fresh new meat trying out for the dance team. As Quincy and the other boys climbed the bleachers, two at a time, causing a disruption to the girl who was in the middle of her routine, he glanced over at Indigo and smiled.

"Hey, Indi, what's up?" he asked.

"Nothing, Quincy, what's up with you?" she said and continued to watch tryouts.

"Just about everybody on the football team nominated you for homecoming queen," he said. "I was the first one."

"That's nice," she said, not even glancing his way. "Thank you."

"I hope you win," Quincy said.

I was sure he regretted dumping Indigo for Patrice Robinson. Indigo Summer had become one of the most popular girls at our school, and Patrice Robinson was just the opposite. She was often referred to as the give-it-up-easy girl, and none of the boys respected her. One man's loss was definitely another man's gain, and Marcus Carter was proud to be the man who had gained Indigo's heart. As he climbed the bleachers and headed toward Indigo, he gave Quincy a cross-eyed look—a look that made Quincy keep moving in the opposite direction.

"What's up?" Marcus asked, and then planted a kiss on Indigo's lips as Quincy watched.

"Been waiting for you," she said, a smile on her face as they gazed into each other's eyes. They acted as if they were the only ones in the room sometimes.

I cleared my throat. "Hello, Marcus. There are other people here."

"Oh, my bad. What's up, Jade?" Marcus said and laughed. "Hey, Tameka."

"Hi, Marcus," Tameka said.

"Was that punk bothering y'all?" he asked Indigo, referring to Quincy.

"He just said that half the football team had nominated Indi for homecoming queen," I said, and gave Indigo a high five. "You go, girl!"

"Of course they did," Marcus said. "Look how fine she is."

He took a seat between Indigo's legs, and all of us watched the rest of the tryouts. It was no secret that all the boys at our school thought that Indigo was fine. I only wished they thought the same about me. But dark girls like me didn't get as much attention. It was always the skinny, light-skinned ones that boys fell over their feet for. Except for Chocolate Boy. He was crazy about me, and I was grateful for that.

After all the routines were completed, Miss Martin's whistle sounded throughout the gymnasium. It became so quiet that you could hear a straight pin fall to the floor.

"Tomorrow morning, a list of those who made the cut will be posted outside the cafeteria," she said. "Good luck to you all."

The girls quietly grabbed their gym bags and other belongings and started moving from the floor. Some of them left the gym, while others decided to stick around and watch the upperclassmen practice. Dressed in shorts and leotards, Indigo, Tameka and I bounced from the bleachers and onto the gymnasium floor. Miss Martin waited patiently as the rest of the team lined up on the floor, and once everyone was present and accounted for, she led us in a medley of stretching exercises.

"I know you girls haven't done a thing all summer to keep your bodies in shape!" Miss Martin said. "Look at you! Your bodies look flabby," she barked and slowly pranced around us, and observed each of us one at a time. "Well, we have a lot of work to do...need to get you all back in shape! Gimme ten suicides."

She blew her whistle, and we all took off running to the other end of the gym, and then back again. My body was worn-out by the third stretch, but I couldn't help gloating at the fact that I had a secure spot on the dance team. The girls that had just left the gym weren't so sure about their futures. Some of them wouldn't be able to sleep tonight from wondering if they'd made the cut. Many of them would be disappointed the next morning when they checked the list, and their names weren't there. I was happy not to be in their shoes.

four

Terrence

MY American history book was the only book I took home, because it was the only class where homework was assigned. My work sheet folded inside the pages, I threw the book against the ripped leather seat. I plopped down in the opposite seat, and then reached over and pulled the window open. It was a hot August day in Atlanta, and I needed a breeze. Just as I leaned my head back against the seat to get comfortable, I noticed LaShon standing over me, her tight Baby Phat jeans hugging her bowlegged figure and her microbraids hanging on her shoulders. Her smile was wide and beautiful as she asked, "Can I sit with you, Terrence?"

"Yeah," I said and stood so that she could slide into the seat next to the window.

She grabbed my history book and handed it to me, and

that's when I noticed that her breasts were way too big for that small top that she had them squeezed into. It was no secret that LaShon had been trying to get at me since freshman year, and I probably would've given her a chance—she was cute, a cheerleader and had a banging body. She was the type of girl that boys hooked up with and kept her around for a while—she was definitely girlfriend material. She was quiet and smart, the kind of girl who would do your homework for you and actually get you a good grade.

LaShon and I never got together because I already had the girl of my dreams—Jade Morgan. Jade, the girl who said exactly what was on her mind, spoiled, hot-tempered. She never did my homework because she was constantly trying to copy the answers from my paper. Jade wasn't as pretty as LaShon, but there was something about her that drew me—even from the moment she walked into Mr. Collins's class, late and flipping him off because he said something about it. Jade Morgan was a trip. She brought out the best in me. Made me want to do better in life, even though she didn't appreciate the great life that she had. Still, she had me striving for more, which is why I couldn't let her know anything about my home life. I couldn't let her know that I was practically raising my brother and sister, and that I was the one who provided a home for them. I couldn't let her know that while she complained about her mother every night on the phone, I wished I knew where mine was.

Jade believed in family—that there should be structure in a home. I guess that's why she was so angry with her parents, because they had decided that they wanted to live in separate apartments. Jade hated that, didn't understand why they couldn't just stay together for the sake of the family. She didn't understand that they were happier living apart, and there was nothing I could say to convince her that she shouldn't let it change who she was. "Don't sweat the small stuff, Morgan," I would often tell her. But she wasn't hearing it. She was hardheaded, thought she had it all figured out. But the truth was, she didn't have a clue. One thing was for sure—she was the type of girl that loved family, and that was the type of girl that you wanted to build a future with. That's if we were old enough to be thinking about a future.

As a high-school junior, I shouldn't have been thinking about a future or anything else that adults thought about, but that was the hand I'd been dealt. I didn't choose to have to take the role of an adult, but Arlene had placed me in this position—with no training, no instructions, no guidance. She was selfish, and some days I resented her. But on days like this one, I missed her. I wished with everything in me that she would be sitting on the front porch when this big yellow bus pulled its wheels up to the curb. I wished like crazy that I didn't have to figure out what was for dinner tonight or that I didn't have to run Sydney a bath full of water before she went to sleep. I wished, just once, that I didn't have to help Trey with his multiplication or fight with him about cleaning up his room before he watched *The Fairly OddParents*. And that's if the cable was still on. Some days it wasn't.

"So what you doin' tonight, Terrence?" LaShon asked.

It was Friday night and most kids my age were going to parties or at least hanging out at the mall.

"*Cleaning the house, starting dinner and getting the kids ready for bed.*" That's what I wanted to tell her. But instead I said, "Nothing. Probably do my homework and check out 106th and Park or something."

"You not going to that party at the skating rink?"

I hadn't even heard about the party, but I didn't want her to know that.

"Nah, I can't even skate," I said.

"I'll teach you how to skate," she offered and smiled. "It's not that hard, boy."

This was the moment that every hormonal boy at my school dreamed of—the day that LaShon Rice invited them to go out. I was hoping that nobody was in earshot when I turned her down. I didn't want people thinking I was soft or a punk. I looked across the aisle at Arthur Jones, whose head was pressed against the back of the seat, his mouth open wide as loud snores escaped from it. I looked in the seat behind me as Kevin Turner bounced his head up and down to whatever he was listening to on his iPod. I looked back at LaShon, her lip gloss beaming against the afternoon sun, like Lil Mama's. She must've snuck and put that on once we were rolling, because I didn't notice it when she first got on the bus.

"Nah, I'ma pass," I finally told her. "I got other stuff to do."

"You still messing with that girl, Jade?"

"Yeah," I said.

"Umm," she murmured and seemed to get an attitude as she tooted her lips and then looked out the window.

Girls were a trip, I thought, as the wheels on the bus came to a screeching halt. I glanced halfway down the block and spotted someone walking from the side of our house. It was hard to make out who it was, as I was the first person to stand. I didn't have time to wait in line. I pushed my way through the crowd and off the bus. Just as I stepped onto the curb, I noticed the perpetrator hopping into his blue and white Georgia Power pickup truck.

"Hey!" I called to him as he pulled away.

I jogged halfway down the block, not really trying to catch the truck—after all, I knew why he had been there. The electric bill was long overdue, and it was too long a stretch between the disconnect date and the day I got my paycheck from Big Tony's. And even once I got my check and cashed it, paying the overdue amount was going to be a long shot. Somehow, I had hoped for a miracle. I had actually hoped that Arlene would've shown up, seen the bill lying on the kitchen countertop—where I'd purposely left it. I had hoped that she would call Aunt Brenda and ask her for a few dollars to pay the bill. But obviously that didn't happen.

I was dreaming, and it was time that I woke up. I stuck my key into the lock, turned it and wished that I didn't have to go inside. Wondered what I was going to do, as I actually tried to flip the light switch on. I already knew that the lights wouldn't come on, but I still felt the need to flip the switch. I guess I needed confirmation as I walked into the kitchen and tried flipping the lights on in there, too. Nothing. No light, except for the sunshine that beamed in through the window over the sink. I pulled the refrigerator open and looked at the food that I'd just bought at Publix grocery store two days ago. I pulled open the freezer and looked at the chicken, pork chops, ground beef and ice-cream sandwiches that were frozen inside. All of it would go bad if I didn't do something quick.

I rushed to the garage, searched through all of the junk on the shelves until I spotted the red cooler—the one that Arlene loaded down with Budweisers and wine coolers when we had cookouts in the summer. It was filthy inside as I carried it to the side of the house, pulled the water hose as far as it would go and filled the cooler with water. Once it was clean, I dragged it into the kitchen and began filling it with meat, ice cream, hot dogs, the gallon of milk and the two-liter bottle of Coke that sat on the top shelf of the refrigerator.

I cut across our backyard and into Julius's backyard, hopped onto his dirt bike, and rode it to the BP gas station around the corner.

"Hey, Terrence, what's going on, man?" Hector asked

as he handed a woman her change. "You not working at Big Tony's today."

Hector had worked at the BP station for as long as I could remember, and over time we had become friends. He was a twentysomething Hispanic guy with a wife and daughter at home. I always thought he was too young to have a family, but who was I to talk. I was a father in my own right, and hadn't even asked to be. Hector often let me pick up a loaf of bread or gallon of milk even when I was short on cash. In return I would take good care of his souped-up Nissan Maxima when he brought it down to Big Tony's to be serviced.

"Nah, I'm off today," I told him.

"I need to bring my truck around there for an oil change. You working tomorrow, bro?"

"Yeah, I'll be there in the morning," I said and dug deep into my pockets. Along with a few pieces of lint, I pulled out two quarters, a dime and a nickel. "I need a bag of ice, man. I'm a little short."

I handed Hector the change. He counted it and then looked up at me.

"Go ahead, man, I got you."

"Thanks, Hector," I said. "Bring me your car in the morning. I'll change your oil and I'll vacuum the inside, too."

I stepped outside the store, grabbed a bag of ice out of the cooler and hopped onto the dirt bike, the bag of ice resting in my lap. I held on to the handlebars tightly and pumped the pedals as fast as I could. If I hurried, I could still fire up the grill before it got dark, and cook enough dinner to get us through the night. I wondered how I would break the bad news to Sydney and Trey, who lived for television and video games. It would be a long weekend without Nickelodeon and BET, but it was the story of our lives. Sometimes we went through hard times. That was just how it was.

I dumped ice into the cooler and on top of the food. I went through the house and opened every miniblind to let sunshine in. I put fresh batteries into my stereo and carried it out to the backyard, set it on the ground and tuned it to 107.9. I went to the kitchen and found a book of matches tucked away in what Arlene called "the junk drawer." It didn't take long to fire up the grill and get the charcoal nice and hot. After the meat began to sizzle, I relaxed in a lawn chair, leaned my head back and shut my eyes.

As I rocked to the music, I wondered if my mother was okay...wondered if she was thinking about us at that moment. I hadn't gone to church that often, except on Easter Sunday and that time when my friend Julius got baptized. And I didn't pray that much, except when I blessed my food from time to time. But today I decided to reach out to the dude in heaven, asked him to look out for Arlene, keep her safe. I also asked him to look out for my brother and sister—and for me. I didn't know if he heard me, but I hoped that he did.

five

Jade

"DON'T even think about touching that door handle, little girl!" I screamed as Mattie raced to the car, a Blow Pop hanging from her lips and a wide grin on her face that I wanted to slap off it.

Once I got close, I grabbed her and tried pushing her out of the way, but she was stronger than I expected. She was stocky, and I had to use my hips to finally push her out of the way and into a small puddle that was left over from the rain, her Blow Pop falling to the ground, and the palms of her hands getting scraped from the fall. You would've thought that I'd slapped her or punched her in the face the way she started screaming for my mother.

"Mommy!" she yelled at the top of her lungs.

I ignored her cries, opened the front door of the car, hopped in the front passenger's seat as fast as I could and stuck the key in the ignition. As soon as I snapped my seat belt on, I started searching for 107.9, Atlanta's hip-hop radio station. Once I heard Chris Brown's voice float through the car, I relaxed. Glanced over at Mattie, who was getting up from the ground, and had real tears in her eyes as she brushed dirt from her hands and knees. She hopped into the backseat of the car, which was where she should've been in the first place. I had already called the front seat and she shouldn't have tried to race me for it.

"I'm telling Mommy as soon as she gets here!" she yelled.

"I told you I had the front seat," I said. "I don't know why you tried to get up here anyway, with your peanut head."

"I bet if I tell on you, you won't be spending the weekend anywhere," she threatened and then topped it off with an insult, "You ugly dog!"

I had already pleaded with Mommy to let me spend the weekend at Tameka's house with Indigo. At first she claimed that she didn't know Tameka or her mother from a hole in the wall, and that I wasn't spending the weekend with strangers. But after speaking with Aunt Carolyn, Indigo's mom, and she told her that Tameka's home was safe, my mother felt better about the situation. All I needed was for my little sister to ruin my weekend for me. I wasn't spending another weekend stuck in my room with nothing to do but watch old DVDs and listen to music.

"It takes one to know one," I yelled back at Mattie. "And if you tell Mommy anything you're gonna get my fist in your face," I said and raised my fist to Mattie. "Now dry your eyes before she gets out here."

She must've taken me seriously because she dried her tears and began to stare out the window. She stuck her thumb into her mouth, a terrible habit that she'd had since she was two years old. Mommy stepped into the car and immediately lit into Mattie.

"Get your finger out of your mouth, Mattie," she said. "I can't stand it when you suck your thumb!"

I glanced at Mattie in the side mirror and watched as she snatched her finger from her mouth and began to pout. I smiled at the fact that she got in trouble instead of me. That'll teach her to stop playing so much.

"Mommy, you got a few dollars for the mall?" I asked. "I forgot to ask Daddy."

She reached into her purse and pulled out a twenty-dollar bill and handed it to me before putting the car in Reverse.

"This is all I have, Jade-bug," she said.

"Thanks," I said and stuffed the twenty into my overstuffed Baby Phat purse.

"Did you straighten up your room like I asked?"

"Yes, ma'am, and I loaded the dishes into the dishwasher, too," I said.

"Good," she said and then headed down Fairburn Road.

My phone buzzed and I flipped it open. A text message from Indigo.

"U on da way?"

"yep." I sent a text back.

"what's ur ETA?" she asked.

"10 min."

"we're goin to da mall when u get here."

"which mall?"

"southlake."

"cool."

Southlake Mall was action-packed when we got there. So many kids from our school were there hanging out and roaming the halls. It was like a big party on a Saturday afternoon.

"I need to go to Charlotte Russe, and check out the clearance rack," Tameka said.

"I need to stop by Bakers and look for some shoes to go with my dress," Indigo said and held her Macy's bag in the air.

She'd found the perfect dress for the homecoming dance, tried it on and it was a perfect fit. I wasn't sure I'd be so lucky. Things didn't fit me like they did Indigo, and it wasn't like I had that much money to spend, anyway. I had fifteen dollars left over from my allowance, and the twenty that Mommy had given me in the car. Whatever dress I found had to cost less than thirty-five dollars or I'd be leaving it right there on the rack. And a pair of shoes was out of the question unless they were free.

I wasn't even sure if I was going to the homecoming dance anyway, at least not with a date. Chocolate Boy hadn't even asked—hadn't even mentioned it, but it was still early. Surely he was planning on asking me—that was a given. Everybody who was anybody was going to the dance and to the football game. Just to be sure, I sent him a text.

"WU?" I asked him.

"U," he responded after several minutes.

"homecoming is next Sat."

"and?"

"and I want 2 go."

"go then."

"U taking me?"

It took a long time for him to respond. So much time, my heart began to pound. I wondered if he had already made plans to take someone else. Surely not. We were exclusive, weren't we? He wouldn't show up at the homecoming dance with another girl when I was his girl. Maybe he had to work next Saturday and wouldn't be able to get off. It seemed that all he ever did was work. But this was important. This was one of those events that you didn't miss in high school. I'd missed out on homecoming last year when my mother up and moved me to New Jersey and I didn't know a single soul there. I wasn't missing out on anything this year. I wanted to be a part of everything.

"yeh…i'm taking U," he typed.

"AIGHT," I replied. He had me nervous at first.

"WUA?"

"da mall. Lookin 4 a dress."

"HF?" he asked.

"ya."

"IMU." He missed me...how sweet.

"ditto," I responded, a smile in the corner of my mouth as I typed the letters.

"call me L8R."

"4sure," I typed and then shut my phone.

I barely heard Indigo as she held a black sexy dress into the air.

"Earth to Jade," she said. "You like this or not?"

"That is so cute, Jade!" Tameka exclaimed. "You should try it on."

Tameka was different now that we were hanging out on the weekend. She usually ignored me, or treated me like the third wheel, as if I was intruding on hers and Indigo's friendship. But today she was different, cool. She had even introduced me in the car to her mother as "my friend Jade." And when we got our nails done at the Asian place, she'd even paid for mine with her credit card. Even though I told her I had it, she insisted on footing the bill for all three of us.

I snatched the dress from Indigo and headed for the dressing room in Parisian's. After slipping it on, I stepped out of the dressing room to show the girls how it fit.

"Now that's cute," Indi said. She looked at the price tag and added, "And it's only $27.99, girl."

It was definitely the right price. And I loved the way it hugged my hips, without making me seem too heavy or odd shaped. I glanced into the double mirrors and checked out my rear end. Not bad, I thought. There was no question that Chocolate Boy would love it, and that was my last deciding factor. I knew the dress would be going home with me as I rushed back into the dressing room to take it off. I slipped it back onto the hanger and got dressed.

Tameka's mother, Mel, picked us up in front of Dillard's. The three of us hopped into the car, snapped our seat belts on and each began bouncing our heads to the Mary J. Blige CD that was playing. I was shocked to discover that not only did Mel listen to Mary J., but she also had Kanye West, Chris Brown and Fabolous in her CD collection. She knew the words and also sang along.

"You girls hungry?" Mel asked.

"We ate at the food court at the mall," Tameka said. "But I could use something to drink, like a strawberry limeade from Sonic."

"Oh, yeah, a watermelon slush would be nice right about now," Indigo added.

"Then Sonic it is," Mel said. "You're right, Indi. That watermelon slush is off da chain!"

I couldn't help thinking how different Mel was from my mother. In fact, they couldn't have been any more different. My mother would never listen to the same type of music as me, and she wouldn't be caught dead sucking on the straw of a watermelon slush. I found myself secretly wishing that Mel was my mother.

SIX

Terrence

My feet were like steel as I lifted them one after the other, the soles of my boots bouncing against the pavement. My hands were still oily from servicing Mr. Charlie's Ford pickup truck. It had taken me the entire morning just to remove his carburetor and replace it with the used one he bought at the junkyard. Removing and replacing carburetors was usually a simple thing to me, but today it was a challenge. I guess my head wasn't in it. I had too many other things floating around in my mind—like figuring out what we were going to eat for dinner, and how I was going to pay the light bill on Monday morning when I had to be at school by seven forty-five and Georgia Power wasn't even open that early. And then on top of that, I'd received a text from Jade, wondering if I was going to take her to the homecoming dance.

Taking her to the dance meant that I had to buy a suit, rent a car and still have money left over to take her out to eat afterward. When she asked, I wasn't expecting the question and it threw me off guard. "U taking me?" Her text still flashed in my head like a bad dream. There was no way I could explain that the homecoming dance wasn't even on my radar—couldn't tell her that I had more pressing issues, like where my family's next meal would come from. She expected an answer, and to say no meant that she might look to someone else to take her, and I wasn't having that. No other dude was taking my woman to the homecoming dance or any other dance for that matter. I didn't care if I had to work overtime at Big Tony's every day this week, I would get the money somehow. Still, the thought of it was weighing heavy on my mind. My back was against the wall, and I needed to do something fast! The dance was only a week away.

"Ain't seen your mama over there in a few days, Terrence. Everything all right?"

Miss Jacobs who lived next door was one of the nicest ladies I had ever met, with her long silver hair that brushed against her shoulders and a face the color of vanilla pudding. She was beautiful for an old lady, and I couldn't help thinking how pretty she must've been when she was younger. I wondered if she had all the men lined up at her door just to take her out on the town.

"Everything's all right, Miss Jacobs."

I couldn't bring myself to tell her that I hadn't seen

my mother in a week and that she'd left us without lights and food. One of my fears was that someone would find out how we were living, and the social workers would come and drag my brother and sister away. I couldn't let that happen. No matter how bad things got, we were a team—we stuck together no matter what. And it was up to me to keep them around, provide for them. That's how it was, and that's how it was going to be. We didn't need an outside source in our family business.

"You know, I cooked this big ol' pot of spaghetti this afternoon. Tried this new recipe that one of the ladies in my bridge club gave me," she said. "I don't know what I was thinking, cooking all this food when it's just me over here." Miss Jacobs laughed and asked, "Why don't you and that little sister of yours...what's her name?"

"Sydney," I said, as I stood on the curb in front of Miss Jacobs's house. She stood on her front porch wearing one of those housedresses that my grandmother used to wear.

"Sydney. That's her name," she said thoughtfully. "She's something else."

"Yes, ma'am, she is."

"Why don't you bring Sydney and your little brother over here later on and help me eat up this big pot of spaghetti?" she asked. "Maybe they can watch cartoons or something, too."

"That sounds good, Miss Jacobs. Let me go over here and get cleaned up, and we might take you up on your offer," I said and smiled and tried my best to be polite. "Thank you for thinking of us."

Might? We were definitely taking her up on the offer for spaghetti. Dinner problem solved.

"You're most welcome," she said and smiled.

It was almost as if Miss Jacobs knew about our home life. Almost as if she knew we didn't have a hot meal waiting for us, or a television that Sydney and Trey could actually turn on to watch cartoons. Still, I had to be careful. Miss Jacobs was nice and all, but I didn't know her that well. And in my neighborhood, you didn't trust everybody. Nothing came without a price. And I began to wonder just how expensive that pot of spaghetti might end up being. It was that thought that had me skeptical about the whole idea all of a sudden. As much as I loved spaghetti, a package of Ramen noodles might be a better choice, considering.

I cut across our yard and trampled up onto the front porch. I stuck my key into the lock but for some reason the door wasn't locked. With caution, I pushed it open, stuck my head inside before entering. The smell of cigarette smoke hit my nose like a freight train.

"How was work?" Arlene asked, a Newport cigarette between her long fingers, and her hair in a wild mess on top of her head.

"It was cool," I said and barely looked at her as I walked past and made my way to my bedroom.

The image of her sitting in that chair in the living room,

leaned back as if nothing had changed, as if she'd been there all week...as if her children didn't need to be cared for...as if the light bill had been paid...as if everything was okay, made me almost lose my cool. Anger immediately overtook me. It was an emotion that I rarely experienced, because I always believed that there was a solution to every problem. There was no need for anger when you knew that. And besides that, I constantly had to remind myself that my mother had a problem—a serious one—and until she resolved it, things would never change.

"Where's Sydney and Trey?" she asked, now standing in the doorway of my room.

"Sydney spent the night at Cee Cee's last night and Trey is over at Miss Irene's. I didn't want to leave them here alone while I went to work today."

"You mad at me, Tee?" she asked.

"Nah," I said and sat on the edge of my bed, kicked my boots off my aching feet.

"You'll never believe what happened," she said and smiled and it was at that moment I realized that my mother's smile had changed. What used to be a bright, beautiful smile was now dull and even ugly. She was beginning to age. She was only thirty-two, but the lines beneath her eyes made her look more like fifty. Her body that was once referred to as a "brick house" by some dude she used to date, was now skinny. She looked sick, and her skin was an ashy brown. And she never took the time to comb her hair anymore. That was the least of her worries.

"Your aunt Brenda play too much. She left the club with some dude that night...you know, the night that I left here...last weekend—said she was coming back to get me in an hour. One hour passed, then two hours. After three hours, I was fighting mad! I was ready to kick Brenda's...well, you know...I was ready to kick Brenda's behind. She didn't even have the courtesy to show back up. So I been stuck over Junie's house all week, which is way over in Decatur. And he kept saying he didn't have no gas to bring me home. People are trifling. I got some words for that Brenda the next time I see her. S'pose to be my friend, but I ain't messing with her no more."

Her mouth was moving, but I was half listening. The stories...I'd heard them all before, and they always ended with, "I ain't messing with Brenda no more..." Her best friend. Her ace. I knew that Brenda would be knocking on our front door before the night was over, and the two of them would be riding off into the sunset in Brenda's Caprice Classic before dusk...again.

"They turned the lights off," I told her. I was sure she'd already discovered it by now, but wanted to bring the matter to her full attention. Wanted to know what she planned on doing about it.

"Yeah, I figured that out when I tried to catch my cooking show just now," she said and smiled that dull smile again. "Boy, you know I love me some Emeril. He be cooking up some stuff!"

I stepped into the bathroom, started the shower. Thanked God for running water. Arlene was right behind me.

"How are we going to pay the bill?" I asked her.

"I already got it covered," she said. "Junie's coming by first thing on Monday morning to take me over to Georgia Power…just as soon as they open I'll be standing at the door."

"And what about dinner today?" I asked. "Miss Jacobs invited us over for spaghetti."

"I thought maybe me, you, Syd and Trey could walk over to the park. Take some hot dogs and hamburgers, throw them on the grill. Feed the ducks and stuff," she said. "What you think about that?"

I knew better than to get excited. Her ideas always ended in disappointment for me, and I wasn't in the mood for hurt.

"Where do we get the hot dogs and hamburgers?" I asked, waiting for her to ask me for a few dollars in order to buy them.

Instead, she flashed an award-winning smile. "I stopped by Publix on the way home. Picked up a few things."

"I'm kinda tired," I said.

"Mommy!" Trey rushed into the house, grabbed my mother around the waist.

"How's my baby?" she asked, and I remembered that once upon a time I was her baby. But that was long ago, and those times were long forgotten. I was a man now, and men weren't anybody's babies.

"I'm fine," Trey said. "Mommy, where you been?"

"It's a long story, baby," she said, and grabbed Trey in a headlock. "I missed you, boy!"

I shut the bathroom door, locked it, got undressed and stepped into the shower. I listened as Trey giggled until he was almost in tears. He was happy to see our mother, but I knew it wouldn't be long before he was sad again, asking when she was coming home. And I'd have to tell him crazy stories until he drifted off to sleep. I shut my eyes as I listened, the water streaming down my face. I had oil underneath my fingernails and all over my hands. I scrubbed until my skin was free from it. The soap was able to wash away the oil from my face and hands. I only wished it could wash away the hurt that tugged at my heart.

seven

Terrence

Hamburger patties sizzled on the hot grill and hot dogs burst wide open from the heat. Trey chased Sydney around the park, holding on to a bug that he'd picked up from the ground to scare her with. Sydney screamed as she took off for the jungle gym. I sat on top of a picnic table as Arlene flipped the burgers. She had found an oldies station on my stereo, and was dancing to a Frankie Beverly tune. I sent a text message to Jade.

"U miss me?" I asked her.

"Lots," she responded.

"Me 2."

"WUA?"

"At da park with my mom."

"Sounds like fun."

"We do stuff like this all the time," I lied.

Sometimes I wanted our lives to be so normal that I would imagine things in my mind. I would imagine that our mother was home all the time, and that every day when we came home from school, she had a hot meal waiting for us. I imagined that we took family vacations together, and watched action-packed movies that we rented from Blockbuster. We did stuff like that when I was younger—when it was just Sydney and me. Arlene would load us up in her Toyota Camry—the one she had before the repo man took it away—and she'd take us to carnivals and drive-in movies. We didn't have money for big vacations, but every now and then we'd drive down to Savannah and go to the beach for a day. And we always had a home-cooked meal, even if it was just Hamburger Helper.

Once Trey came along, things changed for the worse. Trey's father, Bruce, moved away, and it was like Arlene stopped living. She held on to Trey for dear life, like she was trying to relive her life with Bruce through him. It was as if Sydney and I didn't matter anymore. That's when she started caring less about us.

"Wish I were there," Jade's text read.

"Me 2."

"Can't wait to meet UR mom. What's she like?"

"Cool."

"She strict?"

"No."

"Mine is."

"Can't wait 2 meet UR mom," I told her.

"U will...next Sat."

"?" I typed a question mark, wondering what she was talking about.

"Homecoming dance, duh!"

I had forgotten all about the homecoming dance, and the memory of it frustrated me. It was just one more thing on my plate that I'd wanted to forget. But I couldn't because here it was in my face again. The reality of my empty pockets let me know that I had no business with a girl like Jade. She deserved better than I was able to give her. She deserved a real boyfriend. One that could take her to the skating rink on Friday night and to the movies on Sunday afternoon when everybody else went. A boyfriend who didn't have to hold down a part-time job just to keep a roof over his family's head.

"U there?" she asked.

"Yeah."

"My dress is black."

"Gotta go...mom calling me," I lied. Wanted to change the subject as quickly as possible.

"L8R." Her last text bounced across the screen just before I shut my phone. I watched as Arlene took hot dogs from the grill and placed them on a plate, the heat causing the plastic to melt.

"Come on and fix you something to eat, Tee," she said.

I hopped down from the picnic table, grabbed a plate and a bun. She watched as I squirted mustard inside my bun.

Trey and Sydney rushed toward us and Arlene fixed each one of them a plate filled with a hot dog, a hamburger and potato chips. She poured them each a cup of strawberry soda and made them sit down at the picnic table. Trey giggled, mustard smeared across his cheek as he stole Sydney's potato chips when she wasn't looking. I caught Arlene up on everything that had been going on in my life…Jade, the homecoming dance, the geography project that I'd been working on for the past two weeks. She seemed really interested.

"You should be glad to take that girl to the homecoming dance, Tee," she said.

"I am, but I know that it's going to cost me," I told her. "Plus I don't have a car to drive around in."

"You know what?" she asked, stuffing a potato chip into her mouth. "I bet your aunt Brenda would let you borrow her car."

"I thought you weren't speaking to her," I said.

"I'm not. But you could ask her. She would love to let you borrow her car," Arlene said. "You should think about it."

It wasn't a bad idea. Aunt Brenda's car was cool. It needed a good cleaning, and I could shine the wheels a little bit, freshen up the inside. It would work.

"I will," I said. "I'll think about it."

After dinner, Arlene and I gathered the plastic plates and cups and threw them into the trash can. I placed a twist-tie around the bag of hot dog and hamburger buns, and put a clip on the bag of chips. Arlene placed her hand on my shoulder, kissed the side of my face.

"I'm sorry about last week, Tee," she said. "Won't ever happen again. I'm here, and I'm not leaving you guys again like that."

She almost sounded believable, but I was long past believing in my mother. She always said one thing, but did another. My life was filled with broken promises from her.

"You promise?" I knew the truth. She wasn't able to keep a promise if it saved her soul to do it.

"I promise."

I watched as she stuck a Newport cigarette into her mouth, lit it. I didn't know how long Arlene was going to be around this time, so I thought I'd just enjoy as much of her as I could.

eight

Jade

Reclined on a lounger, I twirled my bare toes in the air and slapped away mosquitoes. Sucking on the straw of a watermelon and banana smoothie, I listened to the Quiet Storm on V-103 and closed my eyes as Marques Houston sang. Indigo stared into the sky at the stars, talking about how she used to count them with Marcus at the old airport that he took her to all the time. And Tameka yapped on her cell phone to some boy who was already in his first year of college at Morehouse.

Tameka's backyard was pretty, with lots of purple, pink and red flowers that Mel had planted along the fence. The patio was made of rust and tan-colored bricks, with a table and lawn chairs, and a beautiful umbrella that matched the multicolored pillows. The yard was big enough for a trampoline and a net for tennis, even though it only had a trampoline—the one we'd spent the evening bouncing up and down on until we were exhausted. After we were done bouncing around, we relaxed on the warm concrete, placed cotton between our toes and painted each other's toenails in lime-green polish.

Tameka snapped her cell phone shut. "I think I love him," she said and sighed and held the phone to her chest.

"Does your mom know that he's in college?" Indigo asked.

"If Mel knew he was nineteen years old she would have a cow!" Tameka said. "He's taking me to the homecoming dance."

"For real?" I asked, and sat straight up on my lounger.

"Yes, for real. And I'm going to his, too. At Morehouse," she said.

"Oh my God! Morehouse's homecoming is so hot!" Indigo squealed.

"And the parties that go on at the Atlantic University are off da chain," I added, as if I was an expert on the subject. I had heard some girls talking about it in my literacy class.

"That's exactly why I'm going to Spelman," Tameka said. "There is nothing like the AU—Spelman, Clark and Morehouse—three very hot schools all wrapped up into one little community."

"Yeah, I been thinking about Clark myself," Indigo said. "But I don't know because Marcus is talking about going to some bourgie school like Yale or Harvard. And I don't want us to be too far apart."

"So you might go to school up north?" I asked. I wanted to be sure, because Indi and I had always talked about going to the same college. Since we were ten years old, we had discussed going to either Spelman in Atlanta or NYU. New York just seemed like an exciting place to be.

She glanced my way, realizing what I was really asking. I wanted to know if she was bailing on me, if she'd changed our lifelong plans without consulting with me first.

"I'm not sure where I might go to school," she played it safe.

"Are there any black people at Yale?" Tameka asked.

"A few," Indigo said and laughed. "Very few."

"Where the heck is Yale, anyway?" I asked. I'd heard about the school, but never had enough interest to find out where it was located.

"Isn't it in Michigan somewhere?" Tameka asked.

"No, girl. It's in New Haven, Connecticut," Indigo replied. She had done her research. "And Princeton is in New Jersey. Either way, they're both a million miles away from Atlanta."

"Well, Indi, there's always spring break, the summer and the Christmas holidays," Tameka said.

"I'm sure there are other colleges in Connecticut," I added and laughed. "I have no idea what they could be, but I'm sure they exist."

Who was I fooling? Indi and I weren't little girls anymore, and it wouldn't be long before we'd be considering colleges for real. And there was a good chance that we would choose separate colleges, and I had to accept that fact. If she wanted to follow Marcus around the country, then let her.

"Berkeley College is in New Jersey," Tameka said. "My cousin Janae goes there. She's a sophomore."

"And there's also Rutgers," Indigo said. "I don't know. I'll decide when the time comes. Who knows, me and Marcus might not even be together by the time we both are ready to go away to college."

"Yeah, right," I said. Indigo Summer and Marcus Carter were inseparable, had been since we were freshmen.

"Seriously, Jade. You never know."

"What about you, Miss Thang? Where are you going to college?" Tameka directed her question toward me.

"I don't know. I might go to Howard...in D.C. since Indi's trying to go to Connecticut," I said. "Or maybe New York University."

"What about your little boyfriend, Jade? Where's he going to college?" Tameka asked and continued with her probing into the life of Jade Morgan.

That was a subject that Chocolate Boy and I had never talked about. I didn't even know if he was interested in college.

"I don't know. We never really talked about it," I admitted.

"You better find out, girl. You don't wanna be with somebody who's on a fast track to nowhere," Tameka said.

"It's not like we're getting married or anything," I said.

"True that," Indigo added and gave me a smile to let me know she was on my side. "They're just dating. And who's thinking about marriage, anyway?"

"Brian and I are getting married," Tameka said. "Just as soon as he graduates from med school. We've already talked about it."

"You've already talked about marriage?" Indigo asked.

"You're sixteen," I reminded her. In my opinion, we were all too young to be discussing a subject like that with a boy.

"Still..." Tameka stood, struck a pose and then headed toward the trampoline. "You need to make sure you date people who have their heads on straight. Who has time to waste?"

"That's all we have is time." Indigo laughed.

"I agree," I said. "Let's take our time."

Tameka changed the subject, lightened the heavy mood that had suddenly fallen upon us. "Come on. Let's go for a jump again."

She rushed toward the trampoline, took a plunge and then screamed. Indigo and I couldn't resist and ran toward the trampoline ourselves, took a dive and then bounced into the air. All this talk about college had me really thinking about my future with Chocolate Boy. I suddenly wondered what his plans were for the future, and made a mental note to have that discussion with him. I wondered what my plans were for the future. I wanted to be a lawyer, but it seemed that careers in medicine and law required too much schooling. After you go to a regular college for four years and get your degree, you still have to complete another three years of law school. And you're still not guaranteed anything.

I keep picturing myself in this sexy suit with the cropped jacket and short skirt with a split. I'd be carrying a mahogany-colored briefcase like the one my daddy took to his office. I'd stand in front of a judge and convince him to let some lowlife off the hook because although he'd done something terrible, he still deserved a second chance. The judge would accept my recommendation and the lowlife would pay me a lot of money for getting him off. I'd be the best in my field and everyone would be breaking down the door for my services. Yes…I could see myself as a lawyer. Jade Morgan: Attorney-at-Law. I could see the gold letters on the door to my office—my office with the beautiful view of downtown Atlanta. From my office, I could see the little valet boy parking my champagne-colored convertible Mustang, and I'd be making sure that he took extra care to park it without causing any dings…

"Jade! Did you hear me?" Indigo asked, and I wondered how long she'd been talking to me, because I was a million miles away.

"What?"

"Mel wants to know if you want bubble gum or chocolate fudge ice cream," she said.

I looked up and saw Mel, standing at the sliding glass

door of the patio. I didn't know how long she'd been standing there, but she was holding the door open and awaiting my answer.

"Chocolate fudge," I said.

"Okay, two chocolate fudge and one bubble gum coming right up." She shut the door and disappeared inside.

That day, I discovered what I wanted to do with my life. I wanted to be a lawyer, and with that I bounced into the air. With my life's plans out of the way, I decided to focus on just being a kid.

nine

Jade

After Mel's famous pancake breakfast, it was my daddy's SUV that pulled into Tameka's driveway. My heart was overjoyed when I saw my mother's frame in the front passenger's seat, and Mattie's big head bouncing around in the backseat. Could it be true? Had the three of them spent the night together? Maybe they rented movies from Blockbuster and stayed up half the night talking about getting back together. And now they were just leaving IHOP, where Daddy had ordered his usual steak and eggs, Mommy had ordered bacon, eggs and toast. For the life of me, I never understood why a person would go to the International House of Pancakes and order *toast.* Mattie probably ordered the Rooty Tooty Fresh 'N' Fruity, her favorite, or a short stack of pancakes with strawberries and whipped cream all over them.

As Daddy stepped out of the car, Mattie jumped out of the backseat and followed him to the door. Mel woke us up early and told Indigo and I to get our things together. My bag had been packed all morning. I lifted it and swung it over my shoulder.

"My dad's here," I told Tameka.

"Already?" Tameka asked, disappointed that our weekend was coming to an end.

The sound of the doorbell echoed through the house.

"You think he can give me a ride home?" Indi asked.

"I don't see why not," I told her.

The two of us headed downstairs, our bags in tow. Tameka looked sad that both of us were leaving at the same time. I recognized that look. I felt the same way when friends spent the weekend at my house, and then they had to leave on Sunday. You hated to see them go, especially if you had as much fun as the three of us had over the weekend. We'd done everything from shopping to eating to just hanging out in Tameka's backyard, talking about everything under the sun. We'd redone each other's hair and painted our toenails outrageous colors. Mine were lime green with tangerine-colored tips. Indigo had just the opposite, tangerine-colored nails with lime-green tips. Tameka's were hot pink.

Mel, Tameka's mom, was so cool. I secretly wished she was my mother. Tameka was lucky, and I promised not to make this my last time visiting.

"Uncle Ernest, can I bum a ride home?" Indigo asked my dad.

"Of course," Daddy said, and took both of our bags.

"Can I spend the night next time?" Mattie asked Mel.

"You sure can," Mel said. I hoped she was just being polite, because there was no way my little sister was tagging along on a weekend sleepover with me. I would have to kill her. "Next time I'll make sure the girls bring you along, okay?"

"Yes, ma'am," Mattie answered and smiled. "Thank you."

That was never going to happen, I thought as I ushered her big head out the door. Mommy had her head down as if she was reading something and I wondered why she sent Daddy inside instead of getting out of the car herself. I also wondered what the rest of the day held for us—my family—the Morgans...together again.

Indigo, Mattie and I hopped into the backseat. I made Mattie sit in the middle, which is where she belonged. I shut my door and was about to snap my seat belt on, when I noticed those light brown eyes staring into mine.

"Good morning, girls."

That voice was definitely not my mother's.

"Jade, you remember Veronica, don't you?"

"You mean the Veronica that tried to steal you away from Mommy?" I wanted to ask.

It was her. Again. The woman who my daddy had started dating after Mommy moved to New Jersey. I thought that she was out of the picture. Thought he'd gotten rid of her, but here she was again, all up in the front seat of Daddy's truck. I'd thought she was Mommy sitting there, and that our family was on track again. I'd thought we were getting back together. I should've known better, should've known it was too good to be true.

"Jade, aren't you going to speak?"

"Oh, hi," I said.

"It's so nice to see you again, Jade," the woman said. "You still dancing?"

"Yes, ma'am."

I couldn't believe it. What was she doing here?

"And this is Indigo, Jade's little friend," Daddy said. "They've been friends since...how long y'all been friends?"

"Since second grade," Indigo offered after the words had escaped me. "We lived next door to each other forever..."

"Forever," Daddy said and laughed. "She talks as if they're forty years old, and they're only sixteen."

"Almost sixteen, Daddy. Did you forget how old I am?"

"Sorry, Jade's almost sixteen. She has a birthday coming up in December," Daddy explained.

Veronica laughed. "Very nice to meet you, Indigo."

"Nice to meet you, too," Indi said, and then nudged me. As if I was supposed to say something, too.

I was silent, and stared out of the window as we drove down Jonesboro Road, hoping that Daddy took the quick route to Indigo's house, and then an even quicker route to our apartment. It was too cramped in the car, and I needed some air. I needed to see my mother, and ask her what this woman was doing with my daddy.

When we pulled up in front of Indigo's house, she hopped out of the car and her mom waved from the front porch. I didn't think we would ever make it to her house, but I was so glad when we finally pulled away. I was even happier to see that her daddy's truck was gone. If her dad had been home, there was no doubt that my father would've wanted to stay and talk a while. When the two of them got together and started talking, time stood still. Then Veronica would've been introduced to Indigo's mom, and they might've actually liked each other. That would've been a disaster—especially since my mom and Indigo's mom had been friends forever. They were like sisters, and there was no room for Veronica in that circle.

Daddy rolled down the window and greeted Aunt Carolyn, Indigo's mom.

"Where's that husband of yours?" he asked.

"Oh, he ran over to Home Depot," Aunt Carolyn said. "He'll be back shortly. The game's coming on in a little bit, and I know he wants to see it."

"Tell him to give me a buzz. Maybe I'll come back and watch the game, drink a couple of beers."

"I'll tell him," Aunt Carolyn said. "Thanks for bringing Indi home."

"Anytime," Daddy said.

He waved, closed his window and pulled away. It seemed like forever before we finally pulled into the parking lot of our apartment complex. Mattie had fallen asleep and was already snoring. I shook her.

"Mattie, wake up. We're home."

"We had a late night." Veronica smiled. "We stayed up half the night watching *Ratatouille* and what was that other movie, sweetie?"

Did she just call my daddy *sweetie?* I couldn't believe my ears. That was Mommy's name for him—*sweetie.*

"That big ugly green thing…what's his name?" Daddy asked Mattie.

"Shrek!" Mattie said as she wiped sleep from her eyes. "We watched *Shrek the Third,* Jade."

She told me this as if I cared. I was still stuck on the sweetie thing, and the whole idea of this woman sitting in the front seat of my daddy's truck. Who did she think she was, anyway? And why was she spending quality time with my little sister in the first place? She was temporary. Just as soon as my mother came back into the picture, she would be history again. Daddy would drop her like a bad habit. Mommy and Daddy just didn't know that they wanted each other. We were living in a separate apartment while they sorted things out. There was still hope for a future, and I wasn't giving up so easily.

"Daddy, is Mommy home?" I asked, wanting to bring his attention back to the important people in his life.

"She's gone to church," Daddy said. "So you and Mattie will stay with me until she gets home."

"Yay!" Mattie said, and I wanted to cover her mouth. This was not a happy occasion.

"I have something I need to talk to you and Mattie about, anyway."

Now that sparked my interest. An explanation was definitely needed at this point, and I was all ears.

Daddy shut the car off, and we all followed him up the stairs to his apartment. I went straight for the refrigerator in search of something to drink. I was never sure of what I might find in Daddy's refrigerator. He was a bachelor and rarely went grocery shopping. When I lived with him, there was never any food around either. I just used my imagination most of the time, and ate what was there.

I was surprised to see that the fridge was filled with sodas, juices, Jell-O pudding and all sorts of other things. I couldn't believe that there were three boxes of cereal on top of the refrigerator, and boxes of Little Debbie snack cakes all over the kitchen counter. Even the kitchen décor had changed. There were colorful towels all over the place, and a plant was on the windowsill.

I had been in such a hurry to get to the kitchen, that I hadn't even noticed the changes in the living room. Daddy's old couch was still in there, but it was covered in beautiful pillows and there were candles all over the coffee table. Pictures of Mattie and me were in frames and actually hanging on the wall. And get this…there was an artificial tree in the corner of the room. And the place smelled like Carpet Fresh.

"Wow," I said under my breath.

"Have a seat, Jade-bug," Daddy said. "You, too, Mattie."

The two of us sat next to each other on the sofa opposite my father and Veronica. She sat so close to him, I was tempted to get up and sit in between them. But I resisted the urge, and waited patiently for him to spill his guts.

"I know you girls haven't had a chance to spend much time with Veronica. And I hope that will change. I want the three of you to get to know each other." He grabbed her hand, gave it a tight squeeze. "Especially you, Jade-bug. I want the two of you to become friends."

Now why in the world would I want this woman to be my friend? I had plenty of friends...Indigo...Tameka and a few girls at my school. I even had friends in New Jersey. I was good in the friend department.

"I would like to take you to the studio where I dance, Jade. Show you around," Veronica said. "Introduce you to a few people who I've danced with professionally over the years..."

"My mom sings," I said. I had no idea why I said that, but I just blurted it out. "She sings in the church choir. She has an awesome voice, doesn't she, Daddy?"

"Yes, she does," Daddy agreed.

"Her voice is like Mariah Carey's," I added cheerfully. "Daddy, do you think Mommy is as pretty as Mariah Carey?"

"She's prettier," Daddy said and gave me a wink.

Mattie started giggling. "You love Mommy, don't you, Daddy?" she asked.

"Yes, I do," he said, and squeezed Veronica's hand a little tighter. "I love Veronica, too..."

She had a smile plastered on her face, not realizing that my insides were in turmoil. Did he say he loved her?

"...and Veronica loves me..." he continued, and I wasn't sure I wanted to hear any more. "That's why we are getting married..."

I think my mouth was open. I couldn't tell because I was still in shock. I wasn't sure if I'd heard correctly, and part of me wanted him to repeat the sentence. Another part of me didn't want to hear the words again. So I just sat there.

"You're getting married?" Mattie asked, and at that moment, I knew I'd heard correctly.

"Yes, we are," Daddy said. "What do think, sweetheart?"

"Um, are you gonna have a cake?" Mattie asked the stupidest question I'd ever heard.

"We're gonna have a huge cake," Veronica said. "With lots of flowers on it."

"Can I come to the wedding?" she asked another stupid question, and I covered her mouth so that another one wouldn't slip out.

"What do you think, Jade-bug?" Daddy asked. His big brown eyes stared at me. It was the same look he gave me the day that Mommy kicked him out of the house and he had spent all day loading a U-Haul with his things. He'd looked right at me and asked, "Do you still love me, Jade-bug?"

"Of course I do, Daddy. I will love you always," I'd told him and then wrapped my arms around his neck.

"Will you come and visit me?" he'd asked. "Even though I'm moving, I'm still your daddy."

"And I'm still your daughter," I'd told him.

Here he was giving me that same look. A look that asked for my approval—he wanted me to still love him. He was making this very hard for me. He was asking too much this time.

"I think you're rushing into this," I said. I had to be honest with Daddy. This was too soon. "You don't even know her."

"Of course I know her, baby. We've been dating for more than a year now. I met Veronica right after you guys moved away to New Jersey. She helped me through a difficult time."

"Yeah, but...*we* don't know her."

"You will get to know her," he said. "After the wedding... We're anxious to get on with our lives, baby. And the holidays are coming so quickly, we want to do it around Thanksgiving..."

"Thanksgiving?" I asked. "That's like...November! I thought you and Mommy were working things out..." I grasped for one last straw. I had to keep his attention on the important things...like his children...and the mother of his children.

My phone buzzed and I was glad for the distraction. I looked at the screen and then answered.

"Hi, Mommy."

"How was your weekend at Tameka's?" she asked.

"Good," I said.

"I'm glad you had a good time," she said. "You at your dad's?"

"Yes, ma'am."

"What's the matter? You sound funny." I didn't have the heart to tell her over the phone. I would break the news to her later.

"Nothing's wrong," I lied. "Are you home from church yet?"

"Almost. About five minutes."

"Okay, Mommy. I love you."

"Love you, too, Jade."

I hung up, and stood.

"Come on, Mattie, let's go."

"Wait, Jade, I'm not done here." There was a crease in Daddy's forehead, and he seemed frustrated with me all of a sudden.

I didn't want to disrespect him, but I knew I needed to get out of there—get some fresh air, think things through. This was too much all at once, and I needed to digest it all.

"Mommy's home," I said and pulled Mattie from the sofa and walked toward the door. "Come on, Mattie, let's go."

"I don't wanna go. I wanna stay here with Daddy and Veronica."

"You can't!"

"Yes, she can, and stop pulling on her," Daddy said and

raised his voice, something he rarely did with me and it hurt my feelings.

I didn't wait for another word. I opened the front door and left. Shutting it behind me, I rushed down the wooden stairs, taking them two at a time. My Nine West purse hanging from my shoulder, I walked briskly down the sidewalk, taking in the loud voices and laughter from the kids at the playground. I didn't even look over there, didn't want to stop until I got home. I hoped that Mommy was home by the time I got there so that I could rush inside, run to my room and bury my head underneath my pillow.

Or better yet, maybe I wouldn't go home at all. Maybe I would run far away, and never return. When my phone buzzed, I glared at the screen. It was Daddy. I silenced it and kept moving. When it buzzed again, I looked at the screen again. Mommy. I didn't want to see her, either. I just wanted to be alone, and instead of heading to my apartment building, I moved toward the outer road. I looked both ways before crossing the busy street and then dipped in between a couple of houses.

I remembered Chocolate Boy telling me that he lived near our school, and I headed in that direction. Maybe I would pay him a visit, if I was lucky enough to find the house. I needed to see him. Needed to talk to someone and explain what I was feeling. He could help me sort this out.

ten

Terrence

one more episode of *Hannah Montana* and I was going to climb the wall. I didn't think that my wanting to watch the Wizards put a whipping on the Atlanta Hawks was too much to ask. Sydney had hogged the television all day, and I was just about to claim it back. *Hannah Montana* was about to take a hike.

"Gimme the remote," I demanded, before having to snatch it from her.

"Give it back, stupid," she yelled. "I'm watching this!"

"Too bad. The game is about to come on," I simply said, and then plopped down on the sofa.

Of course, Sydney wasn't going out without a fight, and she lunged toward me. Reaching for the remote control, she landed face-first into the cushion.

"Give it here, Tee. I had it first."

"Too bad, girl. I'm getting ready to watch the game." I pushed her aside as she reached for the remote again.

"You can't just come and steal the television!" she yelled at the top of her lungs, pronouncing every syllable she said. "I was watching *Han...nah...Mon...tana...!*"

Before she could finish her temper tantrum, I had flipped the television to TBS. Just in the nick of time I caught Gilbert Arenas sinking one of his award-winning dunks into the basket. It was nice seeing him back in the game after his knee injury had healed. Sixty-five games were too many games for anybody to miss, in my opinion. But he was definitely making up for lost time. I leaned over, my eyeballs plastered to the screen as I watched the action. I was immediately pulled into the excitement of the game, ignoring Sydney as she stomped into her room and slammed the door behind her.

"Spoiled kid," I mumbled.

The sound of Trey's keyboard caught my attention every few minutes as he worked on some new beats. His latest beat had an Asian twist to it, and I bounced my head as he created it. He was a little genius, I thought as I zeroed in on how the musical instruments came together like a symphony. I crept over toward his bedroom door that was cracked open just enough. I stood quietly outside the door and listened. He was talented—a self-taught musician. I wondered if that would ever mean anything to anyone, and if it would change his life someday.

"I'm going outside, you stupid butthead!" Sydney

yelled as she burst from her room, a bicycle helmet on her head and her bike in tow.

"Stay out of the street," I said softly.

"No!" she said, and then stuck her tongue out at me.

"You better," I warned.

"Make me," she taunted as her neck moved from side to side as she passed by and then struggled to get her bike out the front door.

I held the screen door open for her, as her bike bounced down the front steps.

"I'm not playing, Syd, stay out of the street," I warned again. "Stay on the sidewalk."

She didn't respond, just hopped onto the black leather seat of the bicycle and took off toward her friend Cee Cee's house. I slammed the door shut and found my place back on the sofa to catch the second half of the game. A light tapping on the door broke my concentration and I wondered who would be bothering me at a time like this.

"Who is it?" I yelled, not moving one inch from the sofa.

"Terrence?" a soft girl's voice responded.

I moved toward the door to get a peek through the screen. I was shocked to see the face on the other side.

"Morgan?" I asked, and tried to return her smile.

"Hey, Terrence. What's up?"

"What you doing here?" My heart started beating faster than a normal pace. I was happy to see her, but she caught me off guard. I took in her chocolate-colored skin and the curve of her hips. She wore tight jeans and a snug shirt.

"Looking for you," she flirted.

"Is that right?" I asked, flirting back. "How did you get here?"

"I walked," she said.

"You walked? All the way here from your house?"

"Yes," she said. "Can I come in or what?"

"Yeah. I'm sorry. Excuse my manners," I said and held the door open and checked her out as she walked in. "Have a seat."

She sat down on the sofa, her bottom just barely touching the edge.

"You want something to drink?"

"You got Kool-Aid?"

"Doesn't every black person in America?"

Her laughter filled the room and I found myself smiling too hard. I was grateful to be leaving the room because she had me nervous. Too nervous for someone who was trying to play it cool. Needed to get myself together.

As I reached for a glass from the shelf, a cockroach scurried across the countertop and my heart pounded. I was glad she hadn't followed me to the kitchen. That would've been an embarrassing moment, as I was sure she didn't have cockroaches on her kitchen counter. Funny how they only seemed to play hide-and-seek when you had company.

"I needed to talk," Jade said as she suddenly appeared

in the doorway of the kitchen, and startled me. "That's why I came here."

"That's cool," I said as I rinsed a glass from the sink, and then poured Kool-Aid into it. I glanced in the direction of where the roach had been just seconds before, and exhaled at the fact that he was now in hiding. "What you need to talk about?"

"I just got the worse news of my life," she said.

My heart dropped as I wondered what could be so bad. Had something happened to one of her parents? I handed her the glass and ushered her back into the living room.

"What news?"

"My daddy's marrying another woman," she said softly. "I feel like my life is falling apart."

I didn't know what to say. I knew that her parents were recently divorced and she had lived with her father for a while. I knew that her mother had just moved back to Atlanta. Jade had hopes that they would get back together, but she was upset to find out that they had changed their minds. She took it personal, said that her parents were being selfish. In my opinion, Jade was just experiencing life. If she had to switch lives with me, she would find that hers wasn't that bad after all.

Here I was wondering where my mother was, and how long she would be gone this time. Wondered what I would feed my brother and sister in the meantime. Wondered if the utilities would be shut off this time. After that whole song and dance about not leaving us again, Arlene was gone within hours of us returning from the park. I never believed her promises anymore, because they were always broken. I loved my mother, but I hated this life that she had chosen for us. Jade didn't know a thing about life falling apart.

"Is he marrying that woman you told me about?" I asked. "The dancer?"

"I wonder if she can really dance," Jade said. "She's always talking about it, but I ain't never seen her do nothing."

I almost laughed. She was really hurt about this.

"Come here," I said and hugged her instead. Pulled her close to me. "You'll be okay."

"I just took off running. My parents don't even know where I am."

"You can't run away from your problems, Morgan. You have to face them," I said and pulled her chin up and she actually had tears in her eyes. My heart ached for her. I wiped the tears from her eyes with my fingertips and then my lips found hers. Tasted the Life Saver that she'd just popped into her mouth. My hands crept across her back, as her arms hugged my neck tightly. She felt good in my arms, and I wanted to hold her just like that forever.

The front door slammed against the wall as Sydney burst through it and rushed into the house. She was screaming at the top of her lungs.

"What's wrong with you?" I asked.

Her knee was scraped and blood was trickling down her thin, ashy legs. Her face was soaked with tears and she dropped her helmet onto the hardwood floor.

"I..." she cried and sniffed, "...fell...off...my bike..."

"Come here, girl," I said and ushered her to the sofa. "You just need some peroxide."

I headed for the bathroom and searched under the sink for the brown bottle. I grabbed a dark washcloth and drenched it in cold water. When I returned to the living room, Jade was sitting next to Sydney on the sofa. With her arm around Syd's shoulder, she wiped her tears away. I kneeled and began wiping blood from my sister's knee with the wet cloth. I poured peroxide onto the cloth and dabbed it onto the wounded area. She straightened up and stopped crying.

"Is that better?" Jade asked.

"Yes," Sydney mumbled, enjoying the attention.

"Sydney, this is my girlfriend, Jade," I said.

"Hi," Syd said with her head cocked to the side, checking Jade out.

"Hi, Sydney," Jade said. "Nice to meet you."

"Are you going to stick around for a while?" Syd asked, and I knew where she was going. My girlfriends in the past never stuck around. After they found out that I wasn't able to take them to movies or spend time with them because I worked all the time, they usually dropped me like a bad habit.

"Yes, I'll be around for a while."

“Good!” Sydney declared and stood, placed her helmet back onto her head and rushed out the front door.

I wondered if Jade really would stick around for a while—even after she knew my dark ugly secrets. I hoped so, because I really liked her.

eleven

Jade

The sun was just beginning to set as Chocolate Boy and I walked into the parking lot of my apartment complex. He held on to the handlebars of his brother's dirt bike as we trekked up the hill and past the playground. My heart pounded as I thought about how mad my parents would be at that moment. I knew they'd probably spent Sunday afternoon looking for me and worrying about where I might have gone. I was nervous and wondered if I should head to my daddy's apartment or if I should face my mother first. Either way, I was headed for trouble. I would probably end up on punishment and have my cell phone turned off for a few days. I didn't really expect a whipping, but I wasn't ruling it out. Parents were always full of surprises. I just didn't know what to expect.

"You scared?" Chocolate Boy asked.

"I'm cool," I lied. The truth was I was shaking in my boots.

He wrapped his arm around my neck and pulled me close. "Maybe I shouldn't walk you all the way."

"Maybe you shouldn't," I said and had to agree. I didn't want my parents judging him or turning against him before they had a chance to get to know him.

With that, he propped the bike against a tree, pulled me close. Before I could speak, his lips were against mine—cold and wet. For a moment I forgot about everything. I forgot about the cars passing and the fact that people were probably watching us kiss. I forgot about what happened earlier in the day...about my daddy's announcement. I forgot that Veronica was trying to tear my family apart. I thought she had crawled back under a rock somewhere because my parents were actually starting to love each other again. Then poof, she shows up again. I forgot that I'd run straight out of my daddy's apartment and then found my way to Chocolate Boy's house unannounced. All of those chaotic details began to fade as we kissed. Nothing else mattered at that moment.

"You sure you don't want me to walk you to the door?" he asked after breaking away much too soon.

"I'm sure," I said, my mind drifting back to reality.

"Cool," he replied and let go of my waist. "I gotta get back and check on the two rug rats. Make sure they get dinner."

"Can I ask you something?"

"Shoot," he said.

"Your mom is never there, and you're always babysitting your little sister and brother. Don't you get tired?"

"Sometimes."

"Does she work on Sundays, too?"

"Something like that," he replied. He seemed evasive, grabbed the bike from against the tree. "I'll see you later, Morgan. Text me after you get your whipping."

"Very funny," I said and wasn't smiling.

"Oh, my bad, you probably won't have a phone." He laughed. "Just send me a smoke signal and let me know that you're still alive."

"That's not funny, Terrence."

"I'm just kidding. I hope your punishment is not too bad," he offered and hopped onto the dirt bike and began pedaling out of the parking lot. "I'll see you tomorrow, Morgan."

I gave a simple wave and watched as Chocolate Boy rode the dirt bike down the street. I watched until he was out of sight, then turned and headed toward my apartment building. My feet were heavy as I climbed the wooden stairs.

"Hey, Jade!" Felicia's little brother Jordan said as he came tearing past me and bounced down the stairs with a ball in his hand.

"What's up, Jade?" Felicia asked from behind him, wearing a two-piece red bathing suit and carrying a colorful beach towel. Her braids brushed her shoulders and she pulled them up into a ponytail. "You coming to the pool?"

"Who's over there?" I asked.

"Tasha and Alexis might come. And some of the boys from Hickory Grove might come over and swim today. They were over here last night and we played volleyball with Jordan's ball."

"You're not getting it today!" Jordan yelled as he stood at the bottom of the stairs waiting for Felicia.

"Boy, I'll take that ball from you if I want it," she said.

"Try it, stupid!" He laughed and then took off down the sidewalk.

"Let me go before I have to hurt Jordan," she said and sighed. "Stop running!" she yelled to him. "I'll see you at the pool later, Jade."

I nodded, but didn't really answer. Although it sounded like fun, there would be a slim chance that she'd see me at the pool later. In the midst of all the commotion, I had left my purse at Daddy's and suddenly realized that I didn't have my key to the apartment. I tapped lightly on the mahogany painted door. My mother swung it open.

"Here she is, Ernest," she said and pulled the door open wider so that I could enter.

"Hi, Mommy."

"Don't 'hi, Mommy' me, young lady," she said, not smiling. "Just where have you been?"

My daddy and Veronica were sitting on our couch and stood up when I walked in.

"Baby, I've been driving around all afternoon looking for you," Daddy said. "Where did you go?"

"I just went for a walk," I said. I couldn't believe that the three of them were in the same room together—my mother, my father and my father's girlfriend. What was going on?

"Are you okay, Jade?" Veronica asked. She tried to sound so sincere, but I wasn't buying her little routine. She was the reason for all the chaos in the first place. She was the reason I took off running.

"I'm fine," I said.

"Jade, we've been calling your cell phone like crazy," Daddy said.

"My cell phone is in my purse, Daddy. And I left my purse at your house," I said.

"What are we gonna do about this, Ernest?" Mommy asked. "It was totally disrespectful of her to run off like that. Had us all worried and stuff…I just wanna knock fire—"

"Barbara!" Daddy interrupted. He shook his head no. "We have to handle this in a different way."

Thank God for my father. Had he not been there, I don't know what Mommy would've done to me. I might not have made it through the front door if it was up to her.

"How should we handle it then?" Mommy asked as she peered at me.

"Let me talk to her," Daddy said. "Come on, Jade. Let's step outside."

The two of us stepped out onto the balcony, each taking a seat in the lawn chairs that Mommy had obviously picked up at Garden Ridge or somewhere else over the weekend while I was gone. She'd also picked up candles, rugs and art for the walls. She had our apartment looking and smelling nice. I almost didn't recognize the place.

"What's going on, Jade-bug?" Daddy asked as he held on to my hand. "I know my announcement took you by surprise, but I wasn't trying to hurt you. I just wanted to tell you and Mattie at the same time."

"Why do you have to get married at all? Can't you just date her for a while...just to make sure she's really the one."

"I know she's the one."

"How do you know that?"

"I know because I enjoy being with her. She makes me laugh. She cares about my health, and my well-being. She cares that I spend time with my daughters and tells me that I'm working too much. And I think of her every moment that I'm away from her."

"Even when you were spending time with Mommy—you thought of her?"

"That's how I knew that I was in love with her," he said.

"I don't get it."

"I thought that your mother and I could work things out, and we even talked about getting back together just for you and Mattie. We wanted to do what was right for you two. But what kind of parents would we be if we are miserable together? What kind of example would that be for you?" he asked.

I didn't quite understand, but I let him continue to talk.

"I love your mother, and she loves me, but we can't live together as husband and wife anymore. We don't love each other like that. And we both understand and appreciate that," Daddy said and looked me square in the eyes. "Veronica is a good lady, Jade-bug. She only wants what's best for you and Mattie. And for me. She took a step back to give your mother and me a chance to see if we could make things work."

"She did?" I asked. "And she waited around for you to make up your mind?"

"Well, she didn't really wait around twiddling her thumbs or anything," he said with a laugh. "But I was grateful that she was still there when I made up my mind."

I was a little impressed. From what Daddy said, Veronica sounded okay. I wasn't ready to run inside and throw my arms around her, but it made me curious about her. Made me want to know her better—find out what her angle was.

"That's cool, Daddy."

"I really would like for you to get to know her. Your opinion means a lot to me."

I decided to use that comment as leverage at this point. He needed something from me, and I needed something from him.

"Am I getting a whipping for leaving your apartment the way I did?"

"No. You're getting too old for whippings. You're old enough that we can have conversations like this and come to an understanding. Don't you think?"

"Yeah," I said and totally agreed. "But what about Mommy? She's not always willing to talk. She won't even listen to me half the time. She doesn't even consider what I'm thinking or feeling. She's always ready to just punish me no matter what."

"I'll talk to her."

"I'll probably be grounded two weeks for this one. And will probably get my cell phone taken away…when all I was doing was clearing my head. I needed to think…"

"I understand that, and I'll talk to your mother," he said. "I'll make sure you're not grounded and that you get to keep your cell phone."

"Okay, Daddy."

"But you can't run off like that again, Jade. We were worried," he said. "And you're getting too old for that."

"I know, and I'm sorry, Daddy."

"If you want to be treated like a young adult, you have to behave like one."

"Okay."

"You owe your mother and Veronica an apology, too," he said. He grabbed my hand and pulled me up from the lawn chair. "Come on, let's go inside."

I gave him a big hug and kiss before we went inside. I loved my daddy, and I wanted him to be happy. If it meant I had to spend a little time with Veronica, then I guess I was willing to do that. How bad could she be?

"Love you, Daddy."

"Love you, too, Jade-bug."

* * *

Later that night I wiped dust from my dresser and unpacked my boxes. I placed my little black ceramic angels—figurines that I'd collected since I was three—all over my dresser. I stacked my CDs in the corner of the room and hung my Chris Brown and Usher posters on the wall. Just as I started unloading my clothes from boxes and putting them away in drawers, Mommy walked in.

"I thought you might like this. I had it framed," she said and handed me a silver framed photo of her, Daddy, Mattie and me, a photo we'd taken over the summer at Six Flags. Mattie had chocolate ice cream all over her face and was missing her two front teeth. Mommy and Daddy were smiling as if they were happy, and there was no doubt that I was happy. It was one of the best days of the summer. I remembered it like it was yesterday.

I placed the photo on my nightstand. "Thank you," I said and continued to unpack.

"I know this is hard for you, Jade. But it's really going to be okay," she said. "We're still a family, we just don't live together. That's the only difference."

I nodded a yes.

"Anyway, get your clothes ready for school tomorrow. And don't forget to brush your teeth."

"Yes, ma'am."

After she left, I grabbed my cell phone. Daddy had kept his promise that I wouldn't have it taken away. I sent a text message to Chocolate Boy.

"what U doin?"

"watchin da game...& U?"

"nuthin."

"still got ur phone, huh?"

"and no punishment!" I typed that with confidence.

"got lucky."

"nope...skills."

"whatever."

"thk u 4 being so sweet."

"anytime."

"C U 2mro?"

"at UR locker."

"sweet dreams."

"same 2 u."

I shut my phone, rushed into the bathroom and brushed my teeth. After I picked out an outfit for school, I crawled underneath the covers and tuned the clock radio on my nightstand to V-103. I let the Quiet Storm rock me to sleep, and hoped that dreams of Chocolate Boy would fill my head.

twelve

Terrence

MY Dickies were covered in oil as I pulled the rag from my back pocket and wiped my hands. The last car had pulled out of the garage and I was grateful. Big Tony let the garage down and then locked up shop.

"You did a good job on that carburetor today, son. I know it was a little hard to get to."

"It was all right."

"And I know old man Jenkins ain't the easiest person in the world to deal with. But you handled yourself well," he said with a laugh. "That old man got some issues, don't he, boy? He too old to be driving, anyway."

"You're right about that."

I had a lot on my head, and really wasn't up for all the small talk. I needed to get home and check on Syd and Trey. And I needed to put together a game plan for next Saturday night—the homecoming dance was fast approaching.

"What's on your mind, son? You seem preoccupied." Big Tony knew me too well.

"Same old stuff, just a different day," I repeated his phrase—the one he used almost on a daily basis.

"What kind of stuff?" he asked. "Your mama gone again?"

"More often than not," I said and laughed, but in a sarcastic way. That really wasn't anything new, and Big Tony knew that.

"It's something else then. Something's weighing pretty heavy on you, boy. What is it? Some little girl done broke your heart?"

"Nah, nothing like that," I said. I figured I might as well tell him the truth. "I got this dance to go to on Saturday. Which means I gotta buy a suit…get some wheels…tickets to get in…a corsage for this girl…"

"And money's tight?" It was as if he'd read my mind.

"If I do all that, there's a good chance my brother and sister won't eat for a few days."

"That's some pretty heavy stuff for a young man to be carrying on his shoulders," Big Tony said. "But you're in luck…"

He let the hood down on the old Chevy he had been working on all day.

"What you mean?"

"I know some people," he said. "Come with me."

I followed Big Tony up the flight of stairs and into his small office with the desk that needed to be dusted a long time ago, and the carpet that was covered in dirt and oil—you couldn't even tell what color it used to be. We usually ended the workday in his office—with him reclined in his chair with his boots on top of the desk and me sitting on the opposite side, sunk down in the chair with my hat turned backward on my head. We'd spend at least thirty minutes talking about the jobs we'd completed over the course of the day and discussing everything else under the sun. Big Tony liked to reminisce a lot about his younger days, and I usually just listened.

"I know a little honey that works over at Southlake Mall...at one of the men's stores over there," he said. "She'll hook you up with a nice suit and some shoes...and I'll take care of the bill." He grinned.

"Cool," I said. My shoulders seemed lighter already.

"And tell you what else I'm gonna do for you...since I like you," he said as he removed his feet from the desk and leaned closer in, toward me. Pointing his finger in my face, he said, "I'ma let you get the Cadillac...for one night only..."

Was he referring to his shiny drop-top Caddy with the twenty-two-inch chrome wheels?

"The red one?" I had to ask.

"It's not red, Youngblood. The color is soft burgundy..."

"Oh, my bad."

"...and, yes, that's the one..." he said. "But let me tell you something, son...and listen to me very carefully. If you so much as put a scratch on my ride…I'm talking about the smallest little…tiniest…teeniest…micro…scratch…if you so much as put a ding in my door, or scrape my wheels against the curb…I swear I'll hurt you…"

"Big Tony, I promise I won't hurt your car. I'll take care of the Caddy like it's mine."

He relaxed, leaned back in his chair again and slammed his boots back on top of the desk again. Looked me square in the eyes. "You better guard it with your life, Youngblood."

I was so excited about the car, I could barely contain myself. I didn't want Big Tony to know just how excited I was, because I didn't want him thinking I was too immature to handle the Caddy. Wanted to play it cool, let him know that I was a responsible adult.

"I'll guard it with my life. I promise."

"How much are them tickets to the dance?" he asked.

"Twenty-five dollars each."

"What? It used to be fifty cents to get into the dance when I was your age." He laughed. "Boy, times have changed."

"Fifty cents won't buy you a can of soda anymore, Big Tony," I said.

"You got that right!" he said and laughed as he reached into his back pocket, pulled out his wallet. "Here's fifty dollars, son."

"Big Tony, I can't accept this…I…"

"Oh, what, you thought this was a gift?" he asked, a serious look on his face, a crease in his forehead. "Nah, you gon' work for this. You'll give me an extra hour every week until you pay it off."

There was a long silence between us as I grabbed the bills from him, pulled out my own wallet and stuffed them inside. I was grateful for Big Tony. No one had ever done anything so nice for me. People were always telling me that I couldn't do something, or couldn't have something. It was strange when people did the opposite. I didn't really know what to say.

"Thank you," seemed like the right thing.

"No thanks needed, son," he said and smiled. "You know you remind me of my own son, Anthony, when he was your age? He was just like you—hardworking, honest and responsible."

I was flattered that Big Tony thought all of those things about me. I was hardworking. My grandfather had taught me to be. Said that a man had to take care of himself and his family. "A hard day's work ain't never killed nobody," he'd always said. "And if you want to be a man, you need to work hard and always keep your word. That's the onlyest thing a man has is his word." *Onlyest.* I searched the entire Webster's dictionary looking for that word and couldn't find it anywhere. Grandpa used it a lot. There were lots of words he used that I hadn't ever heard of. Probably because he'd only received a tenth-grade education in school before he had to drop out and get a job. Even still, he was the smartest man I ever knew. Although he passed away when I was in the seventh grade, I still remembered all of our conversations.

Big Tony talked about his son all the time. I could tell that he missed his kids and wished they were still in his life, but his ex-wife had messed that up for him. I think I had become the son that was missing from his life. That was cool, too, because he was sort of like the father I never had. The two of us simply filled a void in each other's lives.

"Get over to the mall tomorrow and get that suit," Big Tony said and stood. "Ask for Rachel and tell her that Big Tony sent you. She'll take real good care of you."

"I will. I'll take the Marta over there after school," I said and stood, too.

"You need a ride home, boy?"

"Nah, I rode Trey's dirt bike," I said.

"So what? We'll throw it in the trunk," he said and pulled a set of keys out of his pocket. "Let's go, Youngblood."

As I sank into the passenger's seat of Big Tony's Cadillac, I took a long look around. The wood grain dashboard was sparkling like the sunshine. The seats were plush, and whatever air freshener he had in there was pleasing to my nose. And when he loaded a CD into the CD player, the speakers were like heaven on earth. Although it was some old-school tune I hadn't ever heard before, I still bounced my head to the music. My mind drifted. In just a few days, I'd be driving this pimp-mobile to the homecoming dance. Jade and I would be the center of attention when we pulled into the parking lot. I couldn't wait. Saturday night couldn't come fast enough.

thirteen

Jade

sitting in front of the mirror in Indigo's room, I carefully smeared gold eye shadow onto my eyelids with a little brush. Indigo put glittered lip gloss on her lips and then brushed her cheeks with something red to match her dress. Tameka placed a stream of freshwater pearls around her neck and then slipped on a pair of strappy, sexy black heels that she'd picked up at Nine West. A toe ring on one of her skinny toes, she strutted in front of the mirror with her hand on her hip. Indigo wiped her lip gloss off and then smeared on a different color. I grabbed Tameka's tube of MAC lipstick and carefully painted my lips gold.

"Let me see that color," Indigo said and then snatched the tube from me. She held it in the air to get a good look.

"That won't work for you, Indi," Tameka said, and then dug down into her little Coach purse and pulled out another tube of MAC. "Try this one."

Indigo grabbed a tissue and removed the lip gloss that she'd just smeared on. She put the lipstick on her lips, smacked them and then looked in the mirror.

"Yeah, that's it," Tameka said. "That's you."

"For real?" she asked and looked toward me for my opinion, too.

"Yep. That's cute," I said and gave her a thumbs-up.

"What about my hair? Is it okay?" she asked. For some strange reason she was nervous.

"Your hair is fine, Indi," Tameka said. "You look cute."

"Why are you so nervous?" I asked as I snapped the clasp on my beaded necklace. "It's just Marcus, and it's just a dance."

"Yeah, but it's our first time going to a dance together," she said. "And plus they named me homecoming queen, so everybody will be watching me."

"That's right! Homecoming Queen Extraordinaire is in the house," I teased.

"And I remember last year when Marcus took some other hoochie to the dance. What was her name, Indi?" Tameka asked.

With attitude, Indigo said, "Charmaine Jackson." She remembered her clearly.

"Charmaine Jackson that lives in the projects with her thuggish, gang-member brothers?" I asked.

"That's the one," Indi said and messed with her hair some more.

"Eeww! One of her brothers tried to talk to me after the game last week," Tameka squealed. "His breath stank and when is he going to get those tired braids redone?"

We all laughed.

"Please don't wear braids if you can't afford to get them touched up," I added. "That is not cute!"

"I remember last year, you went to the dance with that sleazebag Quincy," Tameka said to Indigo. "What a waste of a fly dress."

"I wonder who he's taking this year," I added.

"Probably somebody who's willing to give it up," Indigo said. "It won't be a virgin, that's for sure."

The doorbell rang and we all rushed over to Indigo's window to see if we could tell who it was—to see whose car was outside.

"Who's driving a pimped-out Cadillac?" Indigo asked.

"It's not my Brian. He wouldn't be caught dead pulling up in a pimped-out Cadillac. I'm sure he's driving his mother's Mercedes."

Suddenly, I felt insecure. It couldn't have been Marcus's car—he drove an old Jeep, but had rented a nice Toyota Avalon for the dance. And Tameka's boyfriend, Brian, was not the Cadillac type. He was definitely a Mercedes man. So the only logical choice left was Chocolate Boy—it had to be him sporting Big Tony's pimped-out Caddy. It was a nice car, in my opinion, but suddenly

I felt like an outcast. Indigo must've sensed my discomfort.

"It's a cute car," she said. "I like it."

"Indi!" Aunt Carolyn, Indigo's mother, called. "You girls need to come on down here."

"Coming!" Indigo responded and then turned to us. "Y'all ready?"

"Yep," Tameka said and checked her hair again in the mirror.

"Ready," I said and smoothed the black dress on my hips and made sure my necklace wasn't crooked.

"Let's go."

Tameka and I followed Indigo down the stairs to their family room, where three handsomely dressed young men waited with corsages in their hands. Our mothers were already snapping pictures as we entered the room.

"Mommy, please," I said to my mother, who was wearing a baseball cap on her head because she wasn't able to get to the hairdresser that morning. The first time she meets my boyfriend and she has a nappy head, I thought.

Indigo's mother was dressed in an old pair of jeans and an old T-shirt that had *Jordache* plastered across the front. I'd heard of Jordache jeans, that my mother had worn when she was in high school, but I didn't know they still made those clothes in this century. Mel, Tameka's mom, on the other hand was dressed in a pair of Apple Bottoms jeans and a strapless tube top. She wore bronze-colored wedge-heeled sandals to match her jewelry. Her hair looked as if she'd just stepped out of a hair salon, and her French-manicured nails and toenails were just what my mother and Indigo's mother needed.

"What do you mean, 'please'?" Aunt Carolyn asked. "We have to get pictures."

"Ernest, y'all come on in here and see these girls," Mommy said.

My daddy walked into the room, followed by Indigo's father, Marcus's father and Tameka's father, who I'd only seen for a brief moment at her house when I spent the weekend. He was a music producer, and spent most of his time at the studio. Tameka said that he was gone more than he was at home. But today, he was there with a video camera in hand, capturing the event firsthand. He'd obviously made himself at home with the other two dads, because they all looked as if they'd had too much to drink. Jazz music played loudly on the stereo in the family room and the basketball game was on mute as their conversations grew louder than the music.

Marcus grabbed Aunt Carolyn's camera. "Go ahead and get a picture with Indigo, Mrs. Summer," he said.

"She's not dressed!" Indigo said.

"So what, Indi? Take a picture with your mother, anyway," Marcus said.

"Tell her again, Marcus." Aunt Carolyn smiled. "She thinks she's too cute to take a picture with her mama."

"You can get in there, too, Mr. Summer," Marcus said,

holding the little Sony camera in the air, his finger ready to snap the photo.

Uncle Henry held his beer in the air and didn't hesitate to wrap his arm around Indi's neck. I could tell that she was embarrassed as she frowned at Marcus, gritted her teeth and then reluctantly posed with her parents.

"I don't believe I've ever met you," Mommy proclaimed and turned to Chocolate Boy in the meantime. "I'm Mrs. Morgan."

"Nice to meet you, Mrs. Morgan. My name is Terrence," he countered and shook her hand.

"And I'm Ernest Morgan, Jade's father," Daddy said and took Chocolate Boy's hand in a firm handshake.

"Nice to meet you, sir."

I was grateful that he used his manners when he talked to my parents. They were always watching and judging and one wrong move would tarnish him forever.

"That your Cadillac out there, boy?" Uncle Henry, Indigo's father, asked.

Here goes, I thought. Why did we have to bring up the Cadillac? What difference did it make who was driving it?

"No, sir. A friend of mine, Tony Miller, let me borrow it," Chocolate Boy explained.

"Big Tony?" Uncle Henry asked. "I know Big Tony. He owns that car repair shop over there on Old National Highway. You know Big Tony, don't you, Rufus?"

"Yeah, I know Big Tony. Used to be a professional

wrestler," Mr. Carter said. "I let him do some work on my truck before. Great guy."

"I work for him," Chocolate Boy said. "At the repair shop."

"No kidding?" Mr. Carter asked.

"He must think a lot of you if he let you drive his Cadillac. That's his pride and joy. I do know that..." Uncle Henry added.

"So you have a job, huh?" Daddy asked.

"Yes, sir," he said. "I work there most days after school."

"When do you find time for homework?" Mommy jumped in.

"I find time to do it before I go to bed at night," he said and then looked my way as if he needed me to rescue him. As he held on tightly to the plastic box with the corsage in it, I was sure that his palms were sweating.

"I think it's good for a young man to have a job," Uncle Henry said. "Makes 'em responsible."

"I agree," Daddy said and smiled at Terrence.

"Enough of this talk about repair shops and Cadillacs!" Mel came to the rescue. She gave me a wink and then said, "Let's get some pictures of these pretty ladies and handsome young men together in their outfits and send them on their way."

Our dates placed corsages on our wrists and our parents took pictures until there was no more room on the memory cards of their digital cameras. Finally we were allowed to leave and almost knocked each other over rushing out the door. If they behaved this way just for a little homecoming dance, imagine how they would act when we went to the senior prom.

fourteen

Terrence

Arlene had made me promise to bring my date back to the house before we went to the dance. She'd shown back up just in time to catch me in front of the mirror straightening my tie.

"Where you going?" she'd asked, a Newport cigarette in between her long fingers and a rag tied around her head. She waited for an answer.

"Going to the homecoming dance," I answered and rubbed my palms together and slapped cologne on my neck.

"Where'd you get that suit?" she asked. "You got some money?"

"Big Tony hooked me up," I told her.

"Big Tony this, Big Tony that. You act like Big Tony is your daddy or something. What's up with that?"

"He cares," I said and then left the room. Went to the

kitchen and grabbed a bottle of Gatorade out of the refrigerator. She was right on my heels.

"What do you mean, 'he cares'? You think I don't care?"

"I can't tell, Arlene," I said. "You're never here. We hardly ever have anything to eat. The lights and stuff are always getting shut off. I can't really tell that you care sometimes."

I don't know why I said all of that. I wasn't trying to hurt her feelings, but I was getting tired and frustrated with this lifestyle that she had chosen for us. It wasn't my choice, or Syd's choice or Trey's either. It had been hers. She was our mother, and therefore should've been responsible for us.

"I'm doing the best I can, Tee."

If that was her best, I really didn't want to experience her worst. I envied other kids who worked part-time jobs because they chose to, not because they had to. I wanted to be able to go to the skating rink on Friday nights or to a house party or even a football game at school once in a while. I wished I could play for the team, or even hang out after school and watch them practice. All of my friends either played football or basketball, and I didn't have the time or the money to do either one. Ends had to be met in our house, and I was the one who had to help them meet.

"Are you gonna be here tonight with Syd and Trey while I go to this dance," I'd asked. "If not, I can find them a babysitter. I really don't like for them to be here alone."

"Of course I'll be here," she declared and got an attitude. "I am their mother, you know."

I pushed past her again and stepped out onto the porch, searched for the keys to Big Tony's car. I'd left them on the nightstand in my room. I rushed back in and grabbed them.

"Where you going, Tee?" Sydney asked.

"To the homecoming dance," I said and kissed her forehead.

"With Jade?" she asked.

"Yep," I agreed and smiled at the thought of Jade and took the stairs two at a time. I knew I had just enough time to run by Publix and grab a corsage before picking her up at Indigo Summer's house.

"Who's Jade?" Arlene asked, standing on the porch and taking a puff of her cigarette.

"This girl," I said.

I knew that she was more than just *this girl.* She was someone who I thought about all the time.

"She's his girlfriend," Sydney said.

"Is that true, Tee? You got a girlfriend?"

"He talks to her all the time on the phone," Trey added as he pushed a stick into the dirt and made a hole.

"He sends her text messages," Sydney added and laughed, and then moved her neck with every syllable, "all…the…time…"

"Y'all talk too much," I groaned and unlocked the driver's door of the car.

"I wanna meet her, Tee," Arlene said. The look on her face was sad. She looked as if she'd been left out of a good secret. "Can you bring her by here before y'all go to the dance so I can meet her?"

I looked up at her. Wanted to say no, but I couldn't.

"Please," she whined and sounded just like the mother that used to brush grass from my hair, or put Neosporin on my cuts when I scraped my knee.

"All right," I said, and then hopped into the car. Drove like a speed demon down Camp Creek Parkway with the air on full blast.

Now it was just a matter of breaking the news to Jade, that we needed to take a detour to my house before the dance. I wasn't even sure if Arlene would still be there when I got back, or if she would've taken off somewhere before I had a chance to bring Jade by. I hoped with all my heart that she was still there, because I would be some kind of embarrassed if she had disappeared. I just took a chance.

"My mother wants to meet you and take some pictures of us before the dance," I told her once we got in the car. "Are you cool with that?"

"Yeah, that's cool," she said.

"It won't take long," I promised. "We'll just be in and out."

"Okay," she said softly. "I'm sorry about my parents grilling you like that. Sometimes they really get on my nerves."

"It's cool. I was already prepared for the third degree. They were just being parents," I offered and silently wished I had parents that cared that much about me. "If I had a daughter, I would be the same way if some dude tried to take her out."

"Does your father live in Atlanta?" she asked.

"Nah, I don't know where he lives." The truth was, I wasn't even sure who he was. And whenever I asked Arlene about him, she always blew me off and told me to stop asking so many stupid questions.

I pulled next to the curb, careful not to scrape Big Tony's wheels against the pavement. Aunt Brenda's Caprice Classic was parked in front of the house. Arlene had probably called her the minute I left and told her to come over. She didn't waste any time getting there. Jade sat quietly in the passenger's seat staring out of the window, looking beautiful in her black dress and gold makeup on her eyes. She smiled when she caught me checking her out.

"You ready?" I asked.

"I'm ready."

Before we could step onto the porch, Arlene and Aunt Brenda were outside with their green and black disposable cameras that they'd picked up at Walgreens. They started snapping pictures before we could pose for them.

"Oh, she's so pretty, Tee," Arlene said, and I was grateful that she'd taken a shower and got into some fresh clothes. She had even combed her hair.

"What's your name, baby?" Aunt Brenda asked.

"Jade," she answered sweetly, like she was seven years old. Almost too low for anyone to hear.

"I think the cat got her tongue," Aunt Brenda teased, her miniskirt just barely touching the top of her thigh.

"She said her name is Jade," I responded for her.

"Well, I didn't hear her," Aunt Brenda said. "You shy or something?"

"No, ma'am," Jade answered.

"Don't call me ma'am. I'm still young and tender, honey," she proclaimed and snapped her fingers.

"Leave her alone, Brenda," Arlene admonished and jumped in. "How you doing, baby? I'm Terrence's mother." She tried using her proper English as much as possible.

"Hi," Jade said and took my mother's hand in hers. "It's nice to meet you."

I watched my mother's face soften—a look I hadn't seen in a long time.

"Hi, Jade!" Sydney yelled as she rode by on her pink bicycle with no hands.

"Hey, Syd!" Jade yelled back.

"Hold on to your handlebars, girl!" I hollered, right before she fell onto the pavement. I watched as she got up, brushed the dirt from her pants and hopped back onto the bike.

"I'm okay," she said.

"Tee, y'all stand over there and let me take your picture," Arlene said. "Then, Brenda, I want you to get one of me, Terrence and Jade."

She snapped a picture of Jade and me, and then handed Aunt Brenda her camera. She stood in between the two of us, her arms wrapped around each of our shoulders. She smelled like a Newport cigarette mixed with whatever fragrance she had on. Aunt Brenda snapped a picture with Arlene's camera, and then snapped one with hers.

"We gotta go, y'all. We can't be late for the dance."

"It was nice to meet you, Miss Arlene," Jade said. "And you, too, Miss Brenda."

"You can just call me Arlene," my mother said. "It was nice meeting you, too."

"And I'm Aunt Brenda, honey. Not Miss Brenda—Aunt Brenda. Okay?"

They both were in rare form, making a fuss over Jade like that. I had to admit, though, I was glad they liked her.

I ushered Jade to the car and opened the door for her. After I hopped into the driver's seat, I pulled away—briefly taking a look in my rearview mirror, watched as Arlene and Aunt Brenda waved goodbye. For a brief moment, I had a normal life. Just a brief moment, though. I knew it would be short-lived.

Inside the school's gymnasium, the lights were dimmed, and a disco ball hung from the ceiling. The walls were decorated with black and white crepe paper. People were already on the dance floor funking up their dress clothes as they did the Cupid Shuffle. Jade's girls, Indigo and Tameka, had saved us a seat at their table, and were waving for us to join them.

"What took y'all so long?" Indigo asked.

"We had to go meet Terrence's mother," Jade explained. "She took lots of pictures!"

"Oh, yeah," Indi said. "Parents get crazy with them cameras, don't they?"

"I know," Tameka chimed in. "It's just a homecoming dance. It's not even that serious."

"When we go to the senior prom, now that'll be something to celebrate," Jade added.

The senior prom. I dreaded even thinking about that. If I could just make it through the night, I'd be doing okay.

"Come on, man, let's go get some punch for the ladies," Marcus suggested. "We'll be right back."

The three of us—me, Marcus and Brian—stood, and headed for the punch line. I was grateful to get away from the girlie chatter that Jade and her friends had going on.

"So you playing any sports this year, man?" Marcus asked.

Marcus was an athlete through and through, had been all of his life. Even when we were small kids, he played for the community little-league teams. His father's company name was always plastered on the backs of the T-shirts or on trophies because he sponsored the teams. I always remembered Marcus being good in football.

"I don't really have time right now. Got some other stuff on my plate," I said.

"That's cool," he said. "You know basketball season is coming up. You should go out for the team."

"I'll think about it."

I knew there wasn't much to think about. If I didn't work in the evenings, my family didn't eat. And someone had to help Syd and Trey with their homework, and make sure they brushed and bathed before bed. Some nights I sat up until midnight finishing homework assignments and working on class projects, just so I could make a passing grade. I would love to play basketball for the team. I'd often imagined myself wearing one of the school's jerseys, running out on that buffed floor and bouncing the ball in between my legs before taking it to the hoop.

"I'm the team captain this year, so I got the coach's ear when it comes to who makes the cut or not."

"Word?"

"Yeah, man," he said. "I got you covered."

"That's what's up," I said. "I might just come and check out the tryouts."

"Do that, man," Marcus offered and turned to face Brian, Tameka's college-age boyfriend. "So how do you like Morehouse?"

"Best college in the nation," Brian said. "My whole perspective on life has changed since I enrolled there."

"Spike Lee went to that school, didn't he?" Marcus asked.

"Yep. And Dr. Martin Luther King, Edwin Moses and Maynard Jackson," Brian said.

"Who's Edwin Moses?" Marcus asked.

"He was in the Olympics. African-American gold medalist," Brian boasted.

"Maynard Jackson," I said. "I've heard the name before..."

"Former mayor of Atlanta," Brian said.

"He also helped to rebuild the Hartsfield Atlanta International Airport," Marcus added. "That's why they renamed it Hartsfield-Jackson Atlanta International Airport."

"You know a little bit about your city's history." Brian laughed.

"I know a little something-something," Marcus teased.

"What college you considering?" Brian asked.

"Princeton or Yale, son," Marcus said proudly.

"What? Princeton or Yale. Both Caucasian male-dominated schools. Why?"

"For that very reason you just stated," Marcus exclaimed matter-of-factly. "Somebody has to break down the racial barriers."

"Okay, Marcus." Brian laughed. "What about you, Terrence?"

"You know, I hadn't really thought that much about college. I'll probably go somewhere here in Atlanta, though. Maybe the community college or something."

"Morehouse is always looking for a few good boys...to turn them into men," Brian announced and sounded just like a television commercial. "Seriously, though. You both should come by the campus and let me give you the grand tour. Marcus, you might even change your mind about Harvard and Princeton."

"I doubt it, but I might take you up on the offer," Marcus conceded and poured and filled two cups with red punch.

"What about you, Terrence?" Brian asked and grabbed two empty cups and awaited his turn at the punch bowl.

"I don't mind. I'll take a tour." When would I have time to take a tour? It wasn't as if I had a bunch of free time on my hands. I had made a commitment to play ball and visit a college in less than five minutes, and I wasn't sure how I was going to swing either one of them. No doubt, I wanted to do both.

"Cool. Why don't y'all plan on spending the weekend on campus...in my dorm? I'll show you around campus, introduce you to some people. We'll attend some frat parties. Gentlemen, get ready for the time of your lives," Brian said.

"Sounds like a plan to me," Marcus quickly agreed. "I doubt that I'll become a Morehouse man, but I could definitely check out some frat parties."

"What about you, Terrence?"

Before thinking things through, I had already nodded my head yes, and sealed the deal with a firm handshake.

"Count me in," I said as I poured punch into Jade's and my cup.

I gave her a bright smile when I handed it to her. She smiled back, but had no idea why I was really smiling. She encouraged me to do better things and think better thoughts. Just being around her and her friends had me actually wanting a better future. My little sister and brother needed someone to care for them, but more important than that, they needed a role model. As I took a sip of my punch, I thought, it might as well be me.

Jade and I danced to our sixth song, a slow Chris Brown tune. She placed her head on my chest and wrapped her arms tightly around my waist as we moved slowly from side to side. I kissed her forehead and then her eyes found mine. Her chin rested in the center of my chest as she looked up at me. I kissed her nose, then her cheek and then worked my way to her lips. I kissed her quickly because I didn't want the chaperones walking up on us—teachers and school officials stood in every corner of the room just to make sure nobody got out of control. It *was* a school function, after all.

When the song ended, the lights popped on—an indication that the party was over. I held on to Jade's hand as we crossed the dance floor and found our table. I grabbed my jacket from the back of my seat and tossed it over my shoulder. The six of us headed toward the door and into the parking lot. Leaning against our cars, we began laughing and talking until we finally looked around and the parking lot was empty. A heavy security guard headed our way, no doubt to tell us to move on. We took the hint before he got any closer.

I opened the passenger's door of Big Tony's Cadillac and waited for Jade to hop inside. She kicked her shoes off, and I knew she was more comfortable than she had been earlier.

"Did you have a good time tonight?" I asked as we drove through the streets of College Park.

"Yes," she answered and yawned and then rested her head on the back of the seat.

"What about you, Terrence? It seemed like you had fun."

"It was cool."

What I really wanted to say was that I had the time of my life, but I kept that to myself. There was no harm in holding back a little bit. I gave her a smile as I turned into her apartment complex. I wondered if Arlene was still at home, or if she'd crept out in the middle of the night, leaving Syd and Trey alone in their beds. I wondered if she had fed them dinner or spent time watching the bootleg DVD that I'd picked up at the barbershop the night before. I wanted the night to last forever, because once I pulled up in front of my house, I knew the fairy tale would end. And the night would be a long forgotten dream.

fifteen

Terrence

The porch light was on, and the lamp next to the front door was shining through the miniblinds. I stuck my key in and stepped inside, surprised to find Arlene stretched out on the sofa. She startled me because I wasn't expecting to find her there. I thought she'd be out painting the town red, and I wouldn't see her again for at least a week, and that's if I was lucky.

"Hey, Tee," she said and raised her head when I walked through the door. She was smoking a cigarette and dumped the ashes in an ashtray underneath the coffee table.

"What you still doing up?"

"Waiting for you," she said. "Wanted to hear how the dance went."

"It was cool," I answered and took a seat in the chair

across from her. Kicked my shoes off and loosened my tie and said, "I had a good time."

"I like Jade," she affirmed and smiled. "She seems like a nice girl."

"She is."

"And y'all were clean, too! You all dressed up in your suit and stuff. And that dress she had on...y'all looked really, really nice." She sat all the way up on the sofa and declared, "I got some good pictures, too." She grabbed a cardboard envelope from her purse and handed it to me.

"You got 'em developed already?"

"Yeah! They got that one-hour photo thing at Walgreens, and I made your aunt Brenda run me over there as soon as y'all left."

"Wow," I bellowed and pulled the photos out of their sleeve, began flipping through them.

"Nice, huh?" she asked and smiled.

I had to admit, Jade and I looked good together.

"Yep, they are pretty cool."

It was odd having a conversation with my mother like this—one where she was actually standing still enough to talk to me. Most of our conversations were rushed and usually involved her giving me instructions on what to do while she was out partying. Or they were about me complaining about the lights getting turned off and asking her what she was going to do about it. I was happy that she was home when I got there.

"I really like that one with the three of us in it," she said and took one last puff of her cigarette, smashed it in the ashtray.

I nodded my head in agreement. "Yeah, I like that one, too."

There was silence between us for a moment as I continued to flip through the photos.

"I miss you, Tee," she said seemingly out of the blue. How could she miss me when I was sitting right here in front of her? "I miss you, Syd and Trey. I miss the way we used to be..."

I wasn't sure if she was expecting a response or not, but I just kept quiet, let her finish.

"I'm tired of these streets. Tired of not being here for my kids."

I just continued to listen.

"It took your friend Jade to help me realize that I'm on a fast road going nowhere."

"Jade? What does she have to do with it?"

"You know, when I looked at that girl tonight, I saw myself...twenty years ago," she admitted and laughed a little. "I was a beautiful, smart...young lady. I had so much going for me." Her eyes began to water. "It's just so hard, Tee. When you wanna do right and wrong is standing at your door all the time."

Tears began to fill her eyes, and I went over to the sofa and sat next to Arlene, grabbed her hand in mine.

"Don't cry," I whispered.

"I want to make a change. I know I've made promises before, but I'm really ready this time. But I can't do it by myself," she said. "Will you help me, baby?"

"What can I do?"

"Just be there for me, encourage me."

"Yeah, I can do that."

"I guess the first step is admitting that I have this…this problem. I'm an addict. That's the truth."

By now her face was soaked. I went to the bathroom, grabbed some toilet paper and handed it to her.

"I been looking through these yellow pages," she assented and picked up the phone book that was lying on the floor. "Found a couple of places…you know, those rehab places, where I can go and get cleaned out or something. One of them is like a little halfway house type of setup, where I can stay and work for my rent. And every night I have to attend these little classes and stuff…"

Something inside me exhaled. Her words were like music to my ears. I wanted to cry, too, but I was a man. And men had to stay strong, so that's what I did.

"They do intake on Mondays, so I figured I might go over there and see what they talking about. I can take the Marta train over there in the morning…"

"Can I go?" I asked.

"What about school? You got school on Monday."

"I can miss school that day. You can write me a note and I'll just be absent. I don't have any tests or any projects to turn in," I said. "I wanna go and be there with you."

"For real?" she asked. "You would do that for me?"

"No doubt! I will go with you and stay with you the whole day, until you feel safe and strong enough to stay by yourself."

She didn't say anything, she just wrapped her arms around me and cried. It was hard not to cry, too, but I held strong. Somebody had to hold it together.

sixteen

Jade

We breezed our way through the West End of Atlanta, past the West End Marta station and the Mall West End. Some man was standing on the corner near a gas station peddling oils and perfumes, while another begged for change. Another guy was even laid out on the pavement taking a nap, a dirty and worn backpack next to him on the ground. A boy with his pants just barely hanging from his behind crossed the street right in front of traffic and held his hands out to signal for them to stop. My heart pounded as an eighteen-wheeler nearly sideswiped him. As we sat at the stoplight, someone tapped on the window. We both jumped! Veronica kept her window rolled up, but the man dressed in an old T-shirt and a pair of filthy jeans continued to knock.

"You got a dollar, ma'am?" he asked.

She reached into her purse, grabbed a single bill, folded it and slipped it through a small crack in the window. His ashy fingers grabbed it.

"Thank you. God bless you," he said before making his way to the next car behind us.

The light turned green, and the wheels on Veronica's silver Acura screeched as we went through the light and zoomed down Ralph David Abernathy Boulevard.

I was silent for most of the drive, not really knowing what to say. After all, Veronica and I didn't really know each other. I couldn't imagine what, if anything, we had in common. But she insisted that I spend the afternoon with her, claiming that I would have the time of my life. I doubted that, but didn't want to be rude. And Daddy was just thrilled that we were spending time together. If it made him happy, then I was okay with it.

"I'm glad you were able to come with me today, Jade," Veronica said.

I didn't really have a response to that, so I just smiled and remained quiet, wondered where the heck we were going.

"Have you started planning the wedding yet?" I ventured and decided to break the silence.

"Yes, we have, as a matter of fact," she said. "I'm sorry that you had to deal with all of this so soon, Jade…your parents divorcing and your daddy getting remarried so soon. And you don't even really know me that well. I know that was hard on you."

I nodded my head in agreement.

"I love your father very much, and I'm anxious to marry him" she said. "But...we've decided to move the ceremony to next spring...to give you, Mattie and me a chance to get to know one another."

I continued to listen. I was relieved that the wedding wouldn't be in November as it was originally planned. A lot could happen between now and next spring. Who knew? Daddy might even have a change of heart by then.

"I have a little request, Jade..." she continued. "I would like for you to be in the wedding as one of my bridesmaids. What do you say?"

"I...I don't know..."

"Well, don't answer right now. Think about it, and let me know."

Was she serious? It would be like betraying my mother if I participated in what they thought was a blessed event. I didn't really have to think about it. I already had an answer.

As we swooped past Morehouse College I sat up straighter in my seat. That was the college that Tameka's boyfriend went to, and raved about all the time. He had even invited Marcus and Chocolate Boy to come by and hang out on campus. Once we got to the parking lot, so many people were hanging out in the courtyard—talking, laughing, chatting with one another. Some of them walked past carrying books, while others sat on a stoop in front a café, just hanging out.

"Here we are," Veronica said as she pulled into an empty parking space.

"We're going to Morehouse?" I asked. I was confused.

"No, we're going to Spelman, just up the sidewalk there," she explained and pointed up the hill. "Hope you have on your walking shoes."

It was exciting seeing colleges that you only heard about in conversations or on television. I had lived in the Atlanta area all of my life, but had never visited the AU Center—a place where the historical black colleges of Atlanta were right next to each other. I had never even been to the West End before.

We climbed the hill, Veronica in a pair of sweats and New Balance sneakers, and me in my favorite pair of Ecko Red jeans with the matching top that I got for Christmas last year. I was glad I'd decided on flat sandals instead of the wedge-heeled ones that I normally wore with that outfit.

We stepped inside a building called the Maya Angelou Practice Theatre. Musiq Soulchild's "Buddy" was bouncing off the walls, while five women onstage moved their hips to it. Veronica peeled her jacket from her arms and tied it around her waist. She stepped onto the stage and joined the other women as they practiced a dance routine. She began moving her hips to the music, too. I had to admit, she had rhythm. Just looking at her, I never would've guessed that she could move that way. I sank down into an empty seat at the front of the theater and watched in awe as the ladies swayed to the music.

After they had gone over the routine at least ten times,

one of the ladies stopped the music and they all gave each other high fives. Veronica wiped sweat from her forehead with a small towel and headed my way. Two of the ladies followed her.

"Ladies, this is Jade," Veronica said. "Jade, this is Kenya, my sorority sister and one of my best friends in the whole world. She teaches dance here at Spelman."

"Nice to meet you, Jade," the dark woman with a short natural afro said and took my hand in hers.

"And this is Ilene. She actually teaches literature at Clark."

"Hi," I said softly and shook Ilene's hand.

"She's my sorority sister, too," Veronica said.

"Nice meeting you, Jade. We're glad you could come check us out," Ilene said.

"How do you like our alma mater?" Kenya asked.

The confused look on my face must've let them know that I didn't have a clue what *alma mater* meant.

"Our school," Kenya explained. "We all graduated from here."

"You went to college here? At Spelman?"

"Every one of us," Veronica said. "We were all in the same graduating class. We all took dance and theatre."

Ilene laughed and confessed, "That was many, many moons ago. Long before you were born, I'm sure."

"What grade are you in, Jade?" Kenya asked.

"Tenth grade."

"Have you thought about college?" Ilene asked.

"Um…a little bit," I said.

"We heard that you're a dancer," Kenya said and smiled. "Wanna show us some moves?"

I wasn't sure if I was ready to dance in front of this group of women who had actually taken dance in college. They would critique my moves, no doubt. Several girls who had been standing at the back of the theater suddenly flooded the stage. Each dressed in leotards and dance shoes, they stood in position.

"These are my students," Kenya explained. "Why don't you join them for their next routine. They'll show you the moves."

Ilene pulled me up from my seat and before I knew it I was onstage.

"Ladies, this is Jade," Kenya said. "I want you to teach her the routine until she gets it."

Kenya winked at me, and I smiled. Was she serious? Did she really expect me to learn a routine with these girls?

"Would you like to?" she asked, obviously reading my mind.

"Yeah…I mean…I think so…"

"You can do it," she whispered.

"Are you serious?" I whispered back.

"As a heart attack." She slapped her hands together, and turned toward the stage. "Let's take it from the top, girls!"

There was no time to protest as I was ushered onto the stage and stood in the middle of something like twenty girls. A dark girl with long silky black hair stood next to me and slowly moved her hips while teaching me the moves. It didn't take me long to pick them up and before long we were all moving in harmony to a Beyoncé tune. I wished Indigo could've been there. I couldn't believe they actually had a class where you could learn dance and earn a credit for it. I wanted to grab my cell phone and call Indigo right then, or at least send her a text, but I was too busy shaking my booty.

After we were done, several of the girls shook my hand and told me how nice it was that I could join them onstage. They told me that they would be performing the routine in New York during the Thanksgiving holiday. I wished I could go on the road with them, but knew that was a long shot.

"I'm glad you could join us today, Jade," Kenya said. "Please come back and see us."

Ilene smiled and offered, "Maybe you'll be joining us for real someday."

"Thank you for letting me participate," I said.

The whole day hadn't seemed real.

As I sank into the passenger's seat of Veronica's Acura, I smiled. I didn't quite have words in my head that would describe the day I'd just had, so I didn't try. I just snapped my seat belt on and sat up straight in my seat.

"I like Kenya," I found myself saying as we turned onto Martin Luther King Boulevard.

"I think she liked you, too. She's very strict about her girls, and I've never seen her invite a stranger to participate in a routine."

"That was fun," I said. "And I didn't know you could move like that."

"I still have a little rhythm left in me," Veronica admitted and laughed. "You hungry?"

"Yes," I said. I was starving.

"Good. I know just the place."

She pulled into a tight parking space at a little restaurant on Martin Luther King Boulevard. Several cars filled the lot and people were standing inside. I imagined that the food must've been extremely good the way everyone was cramped inside like sardines. We pushed our way inside the Busy Bee Café, the little soul-food restaurant with a name that described it perfectly—busy. The place smelled of fried chicken, and I could've sworn I smelled peach cobbler, too.

"This is my favorite restaurant in Atlanta," Veronica whispered as we stood just inside the door looking for a table. "Their key-lime pie is to die for!"

We finally lucked upon a table next to a wall filled with pictures of famous people who had eaten there before. Once seated, I scanned the menu and had the hardest time deciding between barbecue ribs and fried chicken, or potato salad and candied yams. I couldn't stop staring at the lady's plate who was seated next to us.

"Have you thought much about what college you want to go to?" Veronica asked.

"Me and my best friend, Indigo, have always talked about going to Spelman or NYU. I'm not so sure anymore because now she wants to go somewhere north," I said. "But after today, I think that Spelman is at the top of my list."

"It's a good school. Has a lot to offer. You might even consider dance and theater as a major."

"Definitely dance!" I interrupted.

"I wanted to major in dance, but my parents gave me so much grief, I ended up with a degree in economics instead."

"My dad has a degree in economics."

"That's right," she agreed. "That's how we met. We worked in the same office until I took a job somewhere else."

The waitress finally approached our table.

"My name is Linda, and I'll be your server today. What can I get you ladies to drink?" she asked.

"Sweet tea for me," I said.

"I'll have a Coke, Linda," Veronica said. "And I think we're ready to order. You ready, Jade?"

"Yes."

"Well, go ahead, give me your order then," Linda pulled out a notepad and a pen.

"I want the barbecue ribs, with macaroni and cheese and candied yams."

"Okay." She wrote it down. "And you, ma'am?"

"Let me get the baked chicken, with black-eyed peas and collard greens," Veronica said. "And we're gonna save room for some of that key-lime pie."

"All right now." Linda smiled and rushed to get our drinks.

I relaxed in my seat, played with the locket that I wore around my neck, twirling it back and forth, back and forth.

"I hope you had a good time today, Jade," Veronica ventured and, cocking her head to one side, smiled.

The truth was I'd had the time of my life, dancing with college students at Spelman College. I didn't want to let on just how much fun I'd had, so I played it cool. Didn't want to give her the satisfaction of knowing that she'd impressed me. That she'd had me thinking more clearly about college than I ever had in my life. That I thought she could dance her butt off! And that I liked her more today than I did yesterday. She didn't need to know all of that just yet.

So I simply said, "It was okay." And then stared out the window of the Busy Bee Café and watched the cars go by.

seventeen

Terrence

AS the Marta train breezed past the Lakewood/Fort McPherson station, I glanced over at Arlene as she sat next to a man who was having a conversation with himself. It was too early for imaginary friends, in my opinion, and I could tell that she was uncomfortable sitting next to him.

"You all right?" I mouthed to her.

She gave me a nod yes. It wouldn't be long before we reached the Five Points station in downtown Atlanta, and she would be free from Mr. Crazy. She held on to her worn-out leather purse and glanced out the window. I knew she was nervous about the whole rehab thing, but she was committed. She was up bright and early in the morning and woke me up.

"You ready, Tee?" she'd asked.

All through the day on Sunday and all through Sunday

night I kept thinking she might back out. I figured that she'd come up with an excuse for not going or would put it off for another week or month. But she surprised me. She was actually serious. After she'd put two ponytails in Sydney's hair and made sure Trey had brushed his teeth, she was tapping on my bedroom door telling me it was time to go. We had walked the two blocks to the Marta station, her gym bag thrown across my shoulder, and I still couldn't believe she was actually going.

The train came to a screeching halt at the Five Points station and the doors opened quickly. Arlene and I hopped off the train and took the long escalator up and ended up on Forsyth Street. She pulled a package of Newport cigarettes out of her purse, lit one.

"You hungry?" she asked.

"A little," I said.

"Okay, let's stop at that McDonald's over there and get a biscuit or something."

"Cool," I said and followed her as we jaywalked across the street right in front of a bus.

People were everywhere downtown, businesspeople and homeless people alike. Businesspeople wearing suits and carrying briefcases walked briskly down the block in order to get to work on time, while homeless people sat curled up on the sidewalk begging for change as we walked past. Several others stood in crowds waiting for their bus to show up, and as soon as the doors swung open a herd of them rushed to get on.

"Can you spare a little change so I can get me something to eat?" a blind homeless woman with a cane asked as she marched up and down the pavement, yelling into the crowd—not really speaking to anyone in particular—just hoping that someone would slip a bill or two in the palm of her hand.

I felt sorry for her and dug deep into my pocket, pulled out a dollar bill and slipped it into her hand. Arlene grabbed the sleeve of my shirt and pulled me toward McDonald's.

"Come on, Tee. You can't feed everybody down here," she said.

"It's just so sad," I declared and looked around at too many hungry faces, and then crossed the street before the light turned red.

Inside McDonald's we stood in a long line, and I glanced at the menu. All I wanted was a sausage, egg and cheese McMuffin, hash browns and a large orange juice. Once we reached the cash register, Arlene told the girl behind the counter—the one with the red extensions in her hair—that she wanted a small coffee.

"How many creams and how many sugars?" she asked in her strong Georgian accent, an impatient look on her face and sleep still in the corner of her eyes.

Were they counting the creams and sugars?

"I don't know, just give me one cream and four sugars," Arlene returned and seemed irritated. "What you want, Tee?"

I told the girl what I wanted, and she rang it up, gave us our total. I reached into my pocket to pull out my last ten-dollar bill.

"I got it," Arlene said, and dug into her purse and pulled out a crumpled-up five-dollar bill and a handful of change. "You've done enough already."

We found a table near the window and my hash browns were gone before Arlene could get all four packages of sugar into her coffee. As she held on to the cup, I could tell that something was on her mind.

"What's wrong?" I asked.

"Just a little nervous," she admitted. "This is a big step for me."

"I'm proud of you."

"That's a trip," she said, and then laughed. "My son is proud of me for a change."

She took a sip of her coffee and I continued to eat in silence.

By the time we reached the rehab center, I was out of breath. We stepped inside the glass doors and checked in with the heavy woman behind the desk. Arlene told her who she was and the woman gave her a ton of papers to fill out. I waited patiently as she completed each form. I smiled when she looked up at me. Wished I could relieve her nervousness, but I didn't know what to say. When she was done, she handed the clipboard to the woman behind the desk. Before she could take her seat again, the woman was ushering her into another room.

"Do you have clothes or anything?" the woman asked.

I handed Arlene her gym bag, and she swung it across her shoulder.

"I guess this is it, kid," she said to me. "You know how to get home on the train from here, right?"

"Rode it a million times before," I told her. "I'll be all right."

Before I knew it, she had me in her arms, squeezed me tight. I squeezed her back, didn't want to let her go. She kissed my forehead and then placed her hand on my cheek.

"I'll call you," she said. "Keep your phone on. I might need you to bring me some cigarettes."

"I'm too young to buy cigarettes."

"There are ways around that," she asserted and laughed and then was ushered away.

She disappeared behind a large orange door, and I stood there for a moment, hoping that she would be okay. I guess she felt the same way back when I was five and she dropped me off in my kindergarten class for the first time. I wondered if it took everything inside her to leave me there, too.

I zipped the front of my hoodie and walked out into the street, headed toward the Five Points Marta station. Past the same crowd of people, and the same blind homeless woman that I'd seen earlier. She was still begging for money. The train was emptier than it was before—the morning rush was over—and I took a window seat. Thoughts of Arlene filled my head, and I wondered if she was for real this time, if she was really going to get it together. I liked being the man of the house, but I wanted to be a normal teenager again and do normal teenager stuff—play basketball or football for the team, go to skating parties, take my girlfriend to the movies or hang out at the mall. When I thought about it, I really didn't have any friends. The friends I used to have were doing normal kid stuff and I was too busy being a grown-up. Before long my head bounced against the back of the seat and I began to doze. When the train reached the College Park station, the doors swung open and I hopped off.

I found myself in the school's gymnasium later that day. Basketball tryouts were underway and I decided to check them out. I took the bleachers two at a time and had a seat. Marcus and a few other guys were shooting around on the court, and when he looked my way I nodded my head. He tossed the ball to one of the other guys and headed for the bleachers.

"What's up, man?" he asked. We gave each other a high five and he said, "You know you need to be down here trying out."

"I'm just a spectator today, bro," I said.

"Why don't you try out?" he asked.

I was dressed in nylon gym shorts and an old T-shirt, and had purposely worn my sneakers. I guess deep inside, a part of me wanted to try out and I dressed for the occasion. I had already told myself that if he encouraged me again, I would accept the offer. And what harm would it do to try out? What was the likelihood that I would make the cut, anyway?

"All right, man," I conceded and followed him down the steps of the bleachers and onto the court.

Someone tossed the basketball to me and I threw a jump shot. Missed. Marcus headed over toward Coach Hardy and spoke with him. Coach Hardy looked my way and made a notation on his clipboard. After that, he blew his whistle and everyone ran toward him. I followed the crowd.

"Let's get started," he began. "I want you lined up single file. You'll take the ball to the hoop in a left-handed layup and then toss the ball to the next guy in line. And when you're done, we'll start the drill all over again, and you'll take the ball to the hoop in a right-hand layup. Got it?"

Everyone just sort of mumbled that they understood and started forming a line in the middle of the court. I stood in line behind a tall freshman, who was undoubtedly trying out for the center position. He missed the left-handed layup and I hoped that I wouldn't miss when it was my turn. When I missed, too, my nerves were on edge. Tall boy missed the right-hand layup, too, and I hoped again that I didn't miss. Fortunately, I sank the ball into the basket with my right hand and caught my rebound, tossing it to the next guy.

Coach Hardy led us through a number of defensive,

passing, dribbling, rebounding and shooting drills. Several drills later, he blew his whistle for the last time and we all gathered around him in a huddle.

"Of course, you know this is the first cut. Tomorrow we'll meet here in the gym at four o'clock and Coach Armstrong and I will announce who made the first cut. We'll repeat this routine again until we get our players down to twelve," he said. "Good luck to you all, and we'll see you tomorrow."

I removed my sweaty T-shirt and wiped sweat from my forehead and underarms. As I moved toward the exit of the gym, Marcus caught up to me.

"You did pretty good, man," he said.

"I did all right. I'm out of shape, though."

"That's all right. Once you make the team, you'll be in shape before you know it."

I found myself actually hoping that I made the first cut. I didn't know where I would find the time to make practice, especially when I had a part-time job and two kids at home. But something inside me came alive when I was out there on the court. I needed to be there—where the action was. I decided that I would find a way to make it happen. *If* I made the team.

I made my way over to the girls' gym, and stuck my head inside. Jade was on the front line shaking her hips to the edited version of Kanye West's "Champion." Her skin was chocolate, silky and smooth. And her hips were perfectly round in the shorts that hugged her behind. I couldn't help staring and my hormones started raging out of control. The more I hung out with her, the more beautiful she became. I wondered if her father would let me take her to a movie or out to eat.

Her eyes locked with mine and I couldn't help but smile. She smiled back, but didn't miss a beat of her routine.

"May I help you, Mr. Hill?" Miss Martin was also my geometry teacher and knew me all too well.

"I was just, um...looking for someone," I said nervously.

"Who might you be looking for?" she asked, and all eyes in the gym landed on me.

"Um...I don't see them in here."

A few of the girls started snickering, and I was embarrassed.

"Well, you can shut the door, please. We're trying to have practice."

"Sorry, Miss Martin," I muttered and shut the door and stepped into the hallway, decided to sit on the stairs and wait for Jade's practice to end.

"Why you trying to bust up in the girls' gym?" Jade teased and laughed.

"I don't know what I was thinking," I admitted and smiled. "I know Miss Martin is strict about that kind of stuff."

"Why weren't you at school today? Were you sick?"

"Nah, I had to do something with my mother," I replied and grinned and kissed her forehead. "Why? Did you miss me or something?"

"A little bit. You could've sent me a text or something, and let me know you weren't coming."

"Sorry. You forgive me?"

"Yes," she asserted and blushed.

I couldn't help but take her in my arms. I had wanted to do that from the moment I saw her. And when she hugged me back, I felt a burst of energy rush through my brain.

"Come on, let's go," I demanded and grabbed her by the hand and led her outside.

I wrapped my arm around her neck as I walked her all the way to her apartment complex.

eighteen

Jade

After my walk home with Chocolate Boy, my head was in the clouds. He had the most beautiful smile and charisma. That was a word that I'd just learned in my literature class—it was one of my vocabulary words. Charisma: *Personal magnetism or charm*—that was the definition, and definitely a word that described Chocolate Boy. I immediately thought of him when I looked it up at Webster online. He was definitely a magnet, because I was drawn to him—and charm, well, he had lots of that, too. I found myself thinking about him in all of my classes. It was becoming hard to concentrate. And I couldn't wait to finish my homework at night and do my chores, just so I could spend the rest of the night talking to him on the phone or sending him a hundred text messages. Sometimes he was really busy, and couldn't talk as much as I wanted him to, but that was mostly because he babysat his younger sister and brother a lot.

His mom was a workaholic in my opinion, and I wished she wasn't gone so much. Because of it, I rarely got to spend any time with him, go to a movie or skating on Friday nights. I usually just tagged along with Indigo and Marcus, and that was boring. Who wanted to be a third wheel?

"Where have you been?" Mattie asked the minute I swung the door of our apartment open.

"I've been at school. What are you talking about?" I quipped and pushed past her and headed for my room, throwing my backpack on the bed.

"What took you so long?" she cried and followed me. "I called Mommy because you weren't here."

"It didn't take me that long! And why did you call Mommy?"

"Because you're supposed to be here when I get home from school. I had to stay here by myself for twenty-nine minutes," she whined.

"So! You didn't die, did you?" I retorted. Still wearing my nylon shorts and a tank top from dance practice, I pulled my sneakers from my feet and slipped on my flip-flops.

"You're supposed to come straight home from dance team practice," she declared. She kept on, "I know you were with that stupid boy, and I'm telling Mommy!"

"Telling Mommy what?"

"That you didn't come straight home and I had to stay here by myself. And I was scared."

I pushed her aside and headed for the kitchen. “Shut up, Mattie. You’re getting on my nerves.”

I grabbed a plastic cup from the cabinet and filled it with sweet tea.

“I’m going to the pool,” I said and stood in front of the door. “You coming or what?”

She thought for a moment.

“What about the dishes in the sink?” she asked.

“Those are your dishes. You messed them up, so you have to clean them up,” I told her.

“And you didn’t clean up your room or put that load of clothes in the washer, like Mommy told you this morning.”

“I’ll do it when I come back,” I answered and stood there impatiently waiting for my second mother—*no, third mother*—to get done with her nagging. “Are you coming or what?”

“No, I wanna finish watching *That’s So Raven.* And then *Hannah Montana*’s coming on.”

“Fine, suit yourself. If you wanna stay here and be scared…”

She thought for a moment again. Fear was a terrible thing in Mattie’s life. I remember when I was her age, I was scared, too.

“Okay…wait!” she exclaimed and rushed into her room, coming back with her flip-flops and goggles.

“You’re not getting in the pool,” I warned.

“Yes, I am!”

“No, you’re not! I’m just going to hang out with

Felicia and them, and I don't feel like watching you while you swim."

"I hate you, Jade."

"I hate you back."

"You stink."

"And you're stupid," I said. "Now come on before it gets dark outside."

Felicia and Angie were lounging by the pool when I walked up. Felicia wore an apple-red bikini as her long brown legs stretched across the plastic lounger. With sunglasses on her eyes and a book facedown on her flat stomach, her microbraids hung on her shoulders. Angie pulled her multicolored sarong tighter around her waist. Her braces seemed to beam as the sunshine reflected on them. Mattie took off for the other side of the pool to play with Felicia's little brother, Jordan.

"What took you so long to get home?" Felicia teased and grinned. "I saw you with Terr-*ence*. Was that a kiss that he planted on your lips, girl?"

I blushed at the thought of Chocolate Boy and the kiss that we'd shared before he took off across the parking lot.

"Y'all are nosy and got too much time on your hands."

Felicia and Angie were the two biggest gossipers in our apartment complex. They knew everybody, and everybody's business. The only reason I hung around them was because Indigo lived too far away. If she lived within walking distance, I wouldn't give the two of them the time of day. But they were somebody to talk to. And somebody was better than nobody. Otherwise I'd be stuck in the house watching *Hannah Montana* with Mattie, and that wasn't even an option. I needed an outlet.

"Somebody said that Terrence's mama is on drugs," Felicia announced. "Said that him and his brother and sister pretty much stay at home by themselves."

"Yep, I heard that, too," Angie chimed in.

"I even heard that he smokes, too," Felicia added.

My heart pounded beneath my tank top, as I wondered if there was any truth to what they were saying.

"Where you hear that from?" I asked.

"He used to date Jasmine Cooper and she broke up with him because he never took her anywhere. Said he was always too busy..."

"Too busy selling drugs," Angie said.

"I thought he used drugs," I said sarcastically, my hands now on my hips as I became defensive. They were talking about the boy who made me smile—the boy that I thought about every day of the week. He was the reason I couldn't get any work done. "Which is it? Does he sell or use drugs, Angie?"

"I don't know what he does, Jade, but you just need to be careful who you hanging out with."

"He seems very mysterious...like..." Angie pointed out and shrugged. "I don't know...like he got something to hide."

"Whatever, y'all. Terrence does not sell or do drugs.

And his mama is not strung out. Y'all got it all wrong," I assured them and plopped down into the lounge chair next to Felicia. "Anyways..."

"Anyways...what's up with your girl Indigo? I heard she was talking to Quincy again," Angie said. "Does Marcus know that she's going behind his back like that?"

That was enough. It was one thing to talk about Chocolate Boy and spread ugly rumors, but Indigo was my best friend for life and they were treading shaky ground by spreading lies about her.

"That is a lie. Indi can't stand the ground that Quincy walks on," I insisted and stood. "I'm out of here. Y'all need to get a life."

"No, she didn't," I heard Felicia say as I walked away.

"Mattie, let's go!" I called out for my little sister and headed toward my building.

Mommy stood with the front door held open when we made it to the top of the stairs.

"Where have you two been?" she asked, a frown on her face.

"We were at the pool," I said.

"I thought I told you that you are not to leave this house before cleaning your room and making sure the kitchen is cleaned," she said. "And didn't I tell you to load those clothes in the washer when you got home from school?"

"I was going to, Mommy, but..."

"When?" she asked. "When were you going to do what you were told, Jade?"

"I planned on doing it when I got home. I just wanted to get to the pool before dark..."

Why was she making such a big deal out of it? It wasn't that serious, and just because she was having a bad day didn't mean that we should have one, too.

"You just completely disregarded what I asked you to do," Mommy admonished. She was angry. "And I'm really getting tired of your attitude and your disobedience, Jade."

"What's wrong with my attitude?" I asked, and wasn't sure if I would survive the question.

"That, right there...that's what's wrong with your attitude."

What was she talking about?

"And then you weren't even home today when your sister got home from school. Where were you?"

"I was at dance team practice and then I walked home from school."

"You were late, Jade," Mommy said. "Where were you?"

I decided to try something new—something that I'd never done before. I ignored my mother, and went into the kitchen, began placing Mattie's dirty dishes into the dishwasher. If she wanted to trip, then let her do it by herself.

"Don't you walk away from me, girl. I'm not done talking to you!"

I kept quiet, and that only intensified her anger. Before I knew it, Mommy was in my face.

"Jade, do you hear me talking to you?"

I walked away and into the laundry room, started loading dirty clothes into the washer. Silently.

"Fine, you wanna ignore me. You go right ahead!" she yelled. I heard Mommy say, "Your cell phone will be shut off before you go to bed tonight. And you're on punishment until your attitude changes...and I mean that..."

I became angry. The thought of not being able to talk on my cell phone depressed me. It meant that I wouldn't be able to talk to Chocolate Boy. I needed to find out if there was any truth to the gossip that I'd just heard at the pool. That was the most important thing at the moment.

"...you hear me, girl?" she asked. "...and I'm calling your father!"

I grabbed my cell phone, just so I could get one last phone call in before she disconnected my service. I knew she would be on the phone with my father for a moment, after which she'd be warming up her computer. It wouldn't take long for her to access the cell-phone company's Web site, where she could temporarily interrupt my phone service with the click of the mouse. I had to move fast. I needed some answers from Chocolate Boy and I needed them tonight.

"Please enjoy the music while your party is located," that was the woman's voice on his cell phone, followed by Lil Wayne's "Lollipop" ringing in my ear.

"What's up, Morgan?" Chocolate Boy asked when he answered.

"You busy?"

"A little bit," he said. "I'll hit you back in a minute."

"Wait a minute!" I said. This was my only chance to ask some questions before I became phoneless. "Got something I need to ask you."

"Make it quick, I'm in the middle of something."

"You know Felicia Clark, right?"

"Felicia Clark…let me think…" he said as he was trying to place her. "She used to talk to Melvin…the dude that flunked the twelfth grade a couple of times. They went to the prom together last year. Felicia…big forehead. Yeah, I know who she is…why?"

"Well, I was out at the pool today, and she was out there with Angie…"

"Morgan, hold on for a minute. I got another call."

Before I could finish my sentence he was on the other line and had me on hold. Didn't he know that I was working on borrowed time, and I didn't have much of it?

When he came back he said, "Okay, I'm back. Now what were you saying about Felicia?"

Dead silence.

"Hello," I said into the phone. "Hello…Terrence…"

Too late. Barbara Morgan was too quick. She'd already shut my phone off, and in midsentence. Sometimes I really couldn't stand her. There were a few dishes in the kitchen sink when she came home, and because of it, she'd gone off the deep end. As if I'd committed a felony or something. The day I turned eighteen would be the day that I moved out of her house. Then Mattie would be stuck with her.

I threw my cell phone across the room, smashed my face into my pillow and groaned. Sometimes life sucked.

nineteen

Terrence

AS I dipped through Mrs. Henderson's backyard, her pit bull, Dexter, started barking his head off. He was going crazy trying to break loose from his chain. I drew closer so that he could see who I was, that I wasn't a stranger. The closer I got, the more his bark became a whimper.

"Chill out, Dex. What's up with you, tripping like that?" I said, actually talking to a dog.

He cocked his head to the side as if he really understood me.

"Where you been, Terrence? Haven't seen you around in a while," Mrs. Henderson asked as she stood in her back doorway, pulling her pink bathrobe tighter.

"Oh, hi, Mrs. Henderson. I've been working a lot lately. Down at Big Tony's Automotive Shop," I explained.

"That's good. Need to keep yourself a job. Nothin'

wrong with a good day's work," she said and smiled and then stepped outside. "Some folks been snoopin' around your house all day. I don't know what they lookin' for…asked me if I knew where your mama was…"

"Oh, yeah?" I asked. My heart began to beat faster than a normal pace.

"You ain't been doin' nothing that you ain't got no business doin', have you?" she asked and raised an eyebrow and looked me square in the eyes.

"No, ma'am."

Were they cops? I couldn't imagine who would be poking around our house…or why. I immediately thought about Syd and Trey and wondered where they were.

"See you later, Mrs. Henderson," I called to her and gave Dexter another rub on the head and took off between hers and Miss Allen's house.

"You be good, Terrence!" I heard her say. "And come take Dexter for a walk sometime."

"I will."

When I reached the front of her house and was facing mine, a dark-blue sedan with tinted windows was parked right out front. There was someone in the driver's seat, but I couldn't make out who it was. I tried to catch a glimpse of the driver as I walked past, and then stepped up onto my front porch. I stuck my key in the door and stepped inside.

"Syd!" I called. "Trey!"

"Tee, where you been?" Sydney asked nervously.

"Somebody's been sitting out in front of our house in that car since I got home from school. I was so scared."

"They knocked on the door, too, but we didn't answer," Trey added.

"Yeah, we're not supposed to open the door for strangers," Syd said. "And I almost dialed 911."

"Sydney called Aunt Brenda," Trey said.

"She's on her way over here."

Both their eyes were as big as saucers as the doorbell echoed through the house.

"It's them again," Trey whispered.

I peeped through the miniblinds and saw a white, blond-haired woman standing on our porch. She wore a navy-blue suit and held a clipboard in her hand. I pulled the door open slowly.

"Hi," she said and smiled. "Is your mom home?"

"No, ma'am," I answered.

"Do you know when she might be here?"

"No, I don't."

Trey and Sydney walked up behind me. I felt Trey's hand grab mine.

"I'm Staci Newland. I'm with Child Protective Services here in Atlanta, and I just have a few questions for your mom."

"Well, she's at work right now. Would you like to leave her a message?" I asked.

"No, I'll just come back a little later when she's home," she said. "Do you know when that might be?"

"Probably not until really late. She works nights, and she's really tired when she gets home. That's why I said you should leave her a message and I'll have her call you," I insisted. I didn't feel right lying about my mother's whereabouts, but I didn't know this woman from a hole in the wall.

Aunt Brenda's Caprice Classic pulled up behind the sedan, brushing the curb. She hopped out, just barely shutting the door.

"May I help you, miss?" she asked, a pair of short shorts sticking to the back of her legs, with a halter top that barely covered her breasts. She held a cigarette in between her fingers, and placed her hand on her hip like she was ready to fight if she had to.

"Hi, I'm Staci Newland," she said and held her hand out to Aunt Brenda, who just looked at her from head to toe and never offered a return handshake.

"Why are you knocking on my sister's door and scaring these children like that, Miss..."

"Newland," Staci repeated. "I'm with Child Protective Services and I'm investigating a complaint that these children have been abandoned."

"Well, as you can see, these children are not abandoned. I'm their auntie...and..."

"And your name is?"

"Brenda. Brenda Duncan."

"You live here?"

"No, I don't live here, but..."

"Is their mother's name..." she inquired and looked at her clipboard, "...Arlene Hill?"

"You asking a whole lot of questions, and not offering a lot of answers," Aunt Brenda said. "Now if you have a phone number where you can be reached, I'll make sure my sister gives you a call when she comes home."

Miss Newland pulled a crisp white business card out of her purse, handed it to Aunt Brenda. "Please have her give me a call," she said.

"I sure will," Aunt Brenda said, and then took a puff from her cigarette. She stood there, intimidating Miss Newland until she headed toward her car. She hopped into the sedan and flipped her cell phone open. I wondered if she was calling for backup as Aunt Brenda ushered us into the house.

I tossed and turned in my bed that night, wondering if Miss Newland was coming back with her posse to take my brother and sister away to one place and me to a different place. I'd heard stories of children being separated and lost in the system, never to find each other again. I was afraid that Sydney and Trey would end up in foster care and I'd lose them forever. That wasn't happening to us. I knew I had to protect my family, but I wasn't sure how that was going to happen before Arlene got herself together. I needed a plan—and fast!

twenty

Jade

I waited as long as I could at my locker for Chocolate Boy to show up. I had about sixty seconds before the tardy bell was due to ring before dashing off to class. I slammed my locker shut, and with my geography book in my arms I jogged through the second-floor hallway. Sliding into my seat just one second before the bell rang, I dropped my book on top of my desk.

It was the one class that Indigo and I shared and of course our seats were right next to each other. Miss Ryan had threatened to separate us in the first week of school, because we had spent most of the period talking and passing notes, but fortunately she gave us a second chance.

"Did you miss the bus this morning?" Indigo whispered.

"Yep, my dad dropped me off. I got in trouble last night, and spent most of it getting lectured," I whispered back.

"Terrence called me. He was looking for you."

"Mommy dearest shut my phone off," I declared and rolled my eyes at the thought of how my mother had completely overreacted.

"I know. I tried to call you last night," she said. "Terrence said to tell you that he'll be here after lunch."

Miss Ryan approached, walking slowly down the middle aisle as she talked about the population of the United States—a topic that I wasn't the least bit interested in. I was more interested in what was going on with my boyfriend. I wanted to know why he seemed so mysterious, and why it appeared that he had some huge secret that he was hiding. I wanted to know why Felicia Clark was going around spreading rumors that Terrence was selling drugs, using drugs or both. *Or* that his mother was drugged out. Where was she getting her information from? But like Indigo's grandmother, Nana Summer, always used to say, "There is some truth to every lie."

Miss Ryan glared at Indigo while she talked, and then glanced over at me. Her body language warned that she was going to move us if we didn't shut up. I sat up straight in my chair and turned my book to the right page, propped my fist against my face. As soon as she walked away, I slowly ripped a piece of paper from my spiral notebook, pulled a pen out of my little Coach purse that Mommy had bought me for my last birthday.

Felicia Clark said that Terrence was a drug dealer and user. And that his mama is on drugs.

I scribbled letters across the page and as soon as Miss Ryan's back was turned away from us I folded the paper and handed it across the aisle to Indi.

U believed her?

Somewhat. Why would she lie?

Consider the source. What did Terrence say?

Didn't get a chance to ask. No phone…remember?

Oh yeah.

She grinned and I shook my head as I folded the paper and slipped it inside my geography book, annoyed that I was having a not-so-good day.

Dance team practice was canceled because Miss Martin had gone home sick. They announced it over the intercom, but I had fallen asleep in my last period and missed the announcement. As a result, I rushed to my locker, threw my book inside and headed straight for the girls' gym. When the place was empty, I couldn't figure out why and decided to search for Indigo or Tameka and find out what was going on. I found them in the boys' gym, where basketball tryouts were going on. Indigo and Tameka sat in the bleachers running their mouths.

"What's up with practice?" I asked as I slid onto the bleacher next to Indigo.

"Didn't you hear? Miss Martin went home with the flu and practice was canceled," Indigo said and smiled. "Look who's here."

I'd totally missed the fact that Terrence was on the

court shooting around with the other boys. Dressed in blue silky shorts that hung past his knees, he shot the ball and it made a swishing sound as it went through the basket. He caught the rebound and then tossed it to another guy on the court.

"I didn't even know he was trying out for the team."

"According to Marcus, he made the first cut."

It turned out that Marcus was right. That was a nice rumor, I thought as I heard the coach call Terrence's name and he joined the other guys on the floor who had also made the first cut. The ones who hadn't made it slowly left the gym with their heads hung low, and their gym bags and wet, sweaty T-shirts flung across their shoulders. I wanted to celebrate with Terrence—making the school's basketball team was a huge deal. The excitement of it actually made me forget about Felicia's rumor. By the time he kissed my lips after tryouts, all I could think of was how proud I was of him.

"You did it!" I exclaimed. "You made the first cut."

"Yeah, the first cut," he muttered and didn't sound as enthused as me. "I still have to make it through the second round."

"And that's what separates the boys from the men!" Marcus came up from behind, placed Terrence in a headlock and they started boxing each other. "You did it, man."

"Yes, I did!" Terrence was cocky now.

All the boys who were in the hallway started chanting, whistling and making loud noises. They were all celebrating their victories. Indigo, Tameka and I looked at each other and smiled. We understood the competitiveness and the excitement of making the cut. It meant more than just being able to dance or play basketball, it meant that you were the cream of the crop.

"Let's all go over to McDonald's and grab something to eat," Marcus suggested.

I immediately knew that wasn't an option for me. For one, I was on punishment until who knew when. Secondly, I didn't have a cell phone in order to call home and beg for forgiveness, and ask if I could hang out. And thirdly, I didn't want to give my mother one more thing to fuss about.

"I can't go," I announced.

"Why not?" Terrence asked and grabbed my hand.

I suddenly remembered that he didn't know that I was on punishment. The phone had gone dead before I'd had a chance to explain what was going on. It also dawned on me that I hadn't asked him about the rumor Felicia was spreading.

"I sort of got in trouble last night. My mother took my phone and put me on punishment..."

"For real?" he asked. "Until when?"

"She didn't say."

"Really? Because I wanted to take you to a movie on Saturday night."

I was amazed, shocked. Terrence and I had never been on a real date before outside the homecoming dance. Never to a movie, or out to eat. My mind started racing a mile a minute, and I wondered how I could get my privileges back by the weekend. It wasn't every day that Terrence Hill wanted to take me somewhere—and I wasn't going to miss out.

"You know, Jade, we still have about an hour before dance team practice is supposed to end," Indigo said. "And your mom doesn't know that it was canceled."

"So technically, you could go with us to McDonald's and your mom wouldn't even know the difference," Tameka added.

"True..." I said thoughtfully.

"Nah, that's not how it should go," Terrence interrupted. "You should go home, Morgan. Do what your mom tells you to do for the rest of the week. That way when the weekend comes, maybe she'll let you go out or something."

He had a point. He didn't know my mother, though. Barbara Morgan—the woman who screamed and yelled first, asked questions later—was not going to be easily convinced that I should go out on a date this weekend. It was my father who was more understanding. Yep, he was the one I needed to work on, and I knew just how to do it. My future stepmother, Veronica...she was the quickest way to my father's heart.

"Yeah, Terrence. You're right. I should go home," I said. "Will you walk me home?"

"Of course," Terrence agreed and smiled and wrapped his arm around my neck.

Terrence and Marcus gave each other dap.

"Congratulations, man," Marcus said. "But it's too early to celebrate. We got another cut tomorrow."

"Yeah, I know. But I'm ready."

"Text me when you get home, Jade," Indigo said. "Oops, my bad…I forgot about your phone."

She laughed and I frowned.

"Ha-ha, very funny," I groaned as Terrence and I walked outside into the fresh November air.

Our fingers intertwined, we crossed the busy intersection on Old National Highway.

"Can I ask you something?" I asked once we got to the other side.

"Anything."

"Felicia Clark said that you were a drug dealer, and that you also smoke weed. And she said that your mama was strung out on drugs," I said. "Is that true?"

"Not all of it," he said.

"You mean some of it is?" I asked.

"A small part," he admitted.

"Well, which part is true?"

We stopped walking for a moment at the entrance of my apartment complex, and Terrence faced me.

"I didn't want you to know, but…I have practically been raising my little brother and sister for the past few years. My mother has been going through some things. It's not her fault, but she just got some heavy stuff going on in her life…"

I didn't interrupt, I just listened.

"Um...she's at this place right now, trying to get clean from drugs. You know, but at least she's trying, right?"

I shrugged my shoulders. I didn't know what to say.

"I work a lot because I have to feed my family...and pay bills. And I'm late for school sometimes because I have to make sure Sydney and Trey get to school on time, and that they have lunch money...and sometimes I spend too much time trying to comb Syd's hair...and..." He stopped, just shook his head. "My life is a trip right now..."

Right then, all of the puzzle pieces came together. All the mystery and the secrets became clear. Terrence always appeared to be hiding something, holding something deep inside. And now I understood. Instead of dating a teenage boy, I was dating a man. And that was scary. I didn't know if I should grab him and pretend to understand, or if I should take off running back to my safe teenage life. My problems were nothing compared to his, and I felt silly all of a sudden—complaining about Veronica and the fact that my mother had shut off my cell phone.

"I've dated girls who couldn't handle my lifestyle. I work a lot, and I got a lot going on. They usually just walk away because it's too much," he said. "And I'll understand if you walk away, too."

As much as I wanted to say, "I won't walk away," I couldn't. Because what I really wanted to do at that moment was run into my apartment and shut the door. My parents had never used drugs before—not that I knew about. Daddy occasionally had a beer with Indigo's father or while watching the game, and sometimes he got drunk. But it was rare. And I couldn't imagine somebody's mama strung out on drugs and leaving her kids to take care of themselves. I felt sorry for Terrence, but his problems were too grown-up for me. I wanted a normal boyfriend—the kind that Indigo and Tameka had. The kind that hung out at the mall and took me skating on Friday nights. Terrence was not who I thought he was anymore.

"I just need to think things through." It wasn't a lie, it was the truth.

"That's cool, Morgan. Get at me when you can."

I felt as if we'd just broken up as he turned to walk away. I watched as he headed down the block, his gym bag tossed across his shoulder, his head hung as he crossed Old National Highway.

Something had changed.

twenty-one

Terrence

BY the time I hopped off the Marta train at the Five Points station, three people had already asked me for a dollar. I took the escalator up to Forsyth Street in downtown Atlanta and jaywalked in the middle of the street. Today was a good day, I thought as the city bus just missed me before I stepped up onto the curb. Much better than yesterday, when Morgan had done what everyone else in my life had done—walked away. I had told myself that she was different, but instead she turned out to be just like all the rest. Shallow. Childish. She was avoiding me at school, and dodged me after her dance team practice—claiming that her father was picking her up and she didn't need me to walk her home. It was cool. She wasn't the first girl to walk away, and she probably wouldn't be the last. Who was I to think that I could have a real girlfriend, anyway? Too much drama, and I had enough on my plate.

That was yesterday. Today was much better.

Today, Coach Hardy had called my name for the second time, and I was officially a bona fide member of the school's basketball team. I had never been a part of anything with structure—never played little league, never went to summer camp. I occasionally went on field trips when I was small, but only if it didn't cost Arlene any money to send me. It was exciting being a part of something, and I wanted to shout it to the world. I had already dropped by Big Tony's and told him about it—let him know that I would have to scale back on my hours at the shop so that I could make it to basketball practice every day.

"That's good, son, I'm proud of you," Big Tony had said. "And don't worry about your hours at the shop. I'm going to pay you the same salary as if you were here. How you like that?"

I liked it a lot, and I tried to contain my excitement about it until I was out of his presence. I wanted to hug him, but I didn't. Wasn't sure how he might react. Men just didn't go around hugging each other like that, so I just gave him a handshake and told him thanks.

I couldn't wait to tell Arlene my news as I stepped inside the glass doors at the rehab center and greeted the receptionist.

"I'm here to see Arlene Hill, please," I said.

She flipped through the stack of papers on her desk and

found a list—a list that probably held the names of people's mothers, fathers, aunties and cousins who couldn't find freedom from drugs and alcohol on their own, so they wound up in a place like this to get help.

After she looked for Arlene's name on the list, the woman looked up and said, "She's not here anymore. She left this morning."

I was shocked. What did she mean Arlene wasn't there? Wasn't this a thirty-day program?

"I don't understand. I dropped her off here last week, and I talked to her on the phone just yesterday."

"I'm sorry, she left this morning, honey."

She repeated the words, but I wasn't sure if I heard her clearly even for the second time. My shock turned into anger. How could she just give up like that? I thought she was in the program to get clean—so that she could be a better mother and take care of us like she was supposed to. What happened to that? What happened to all the promises she made? I believed her—believed that she was serious this time. But I guess she didn't love us as much as she claimed she did. She didn't love us enough to even try.

In my book, she was a loser.

"Thank you," I mumbled before walking through the glass doors again and into the hallway. I wanted to punch something. My head hung low, I stepped out into the brisk air, threw my hoodie on my head and headed toward the train station.

* * *

I stepped upon to the porch, unlocked the door. I froze at the complete silence in the house—no *Hannah Montana* blaring from the television, no music from Trey's room as he created his beats. They were gone, and I immediately thought of Miss Newland from Child Protective Services, driving the blue sedan with tinted windows. She'd found us out and taken them away. They would be placed in foster care and I would never see them again. I checked their rooms—knowing they weren't there, but I needed to check, anyway. Each room was empty, just as I thought. I walked outside, looked up the block toward Cee Cee's house and then down the other way. No sign of them anywhere. I rushed next door and banged on Miss Jacobs's door.

"Hello, Terrence. Is everything all right?"

"Miss Jacobs, have you seen my brother and sister? They're not at home, and I don't know where they went!"

"No, baby. I'm sorry, I haven't seen them. I just got home about twenty minutes ago. Had to go to the doctor's office and then to pick up my prescriptions from the pharmacy. Doctor said my blood pressure is through the roof—said I need to quit eatin' so much pork..."

I was becoming impatient with Miss Jacobs as she gave me a rundown of all of her ailments. I was trying to use my manners and not be rude, but that was a hard thing to do whenever Miss Jacobs started talking.

"Thank you, Miss Jacobs. I'll see you later," I said and worked my way down the stairs and off her porch.

I didn't know which way to turn or where to look. As I sat on the front steps, the cool air blowing against my face, I pulled my cell phone out of my pocket and looked for Aunt Brenda's name in my address book. Prayed that Sydney and Trey were with her, or that she at least knew where they were. Or at least where Arlene was. When I reached her voice mail, everything in me seemed to die a slow death. I was all they had, and I had blown it. I sat there for a moment, a million thoughts rushing through my head. I wondered exactly where I could find the office of Child Protective Services and how I would get there. But then I thought, what would I do once I got there? Demand that they give my sister and brother back to me?

"You're a minor yourself, Terrence," I whispered to myself.

They would probably even take me into custody, not that anyone would take me into foster care or adopt me. I was too old, and I had heard stories about kids my age being lost in the system.

The sound of a Jill Scott tune rang through the streets before I even noticed Aunt Brenda's car pull up. She blew the horn to let me know it was her. I lifted my head and then stood. Arlene stepped out of the passenger's side of the car. Sydney and Trey jumped out the backseat and ran toward the house.

"Tee, we went to CiCi's Pizza!" Trey yelled.

"We brought you some pizza," Syd said and handed me

a carton of food, and followed Trey into the house. "It's got pineapples on it!" she yelled before slamming the door.

I was so happy to see them, I wanted to leap for joy. Instead I turned toward Arlene.

"Why didn't you tell me that you left the center?" I asked her.

"I'm sorry, Tee. After Brenda told me about that woman from CPS sniffing around here, I had to come and check on my kids."

"I was worried," I said. "I didn't know what happened to Syd and Trey. When I came home from school and they weren't here..."

"I know, baby. I should've called you on your cell phone and let you know. But I had Brenda pick me up first thing this morning and I went right over to that office to straighten things out. Let them know they weren't taking my kids nowhere."

"What about your treatment and your thirty-day clean-up period? Did you give up?" I asked.

"No, Tee. I didn't give up." She smiled. "But I think I can do this on my own."

"I don't know, Arlene. If you could do it on your own, you would've done it a long time ago."

"I'm motivated to succeed now."

"What's your motivation now that wasn't there before?"

"You." She smiled. "Seeing you working so hard to take care of your brother and sister let me know that I was half stepping on my responsibility. And seeing you with Jade that day. I knew that I wanted to be a part of many more events like that in your life, Tee. You've grown up on me—right before my eyes—and I haven't even been around. I don't wanna miss anything else..."

Aunt Brenda stepped out of the car to see what we were talking about. She stood by while Arlene continued to spill her guts.

"...and Syd is growing up to be a young lady. She needs me. She needs a mother."

"So you're gonna continue with the classes that you said you like so much? The alcohol and drug classes?"

"Every Tuesday night," she said. "Brenda's gonna come by and pick me up and take me."

"That's right," Aunt Brenda said.

I wanted to ask if Aunt Brenda was going to attend the classes with Arlene. It was no secret that she had some of the same problems—maybe not as bad—but similar.

"I might even go myself, Tee." She grinned. "Can you get with that?"

"I can get with that."

"It's cold out here, boy. Let's go inside and you can warm up your pizza," Arlene offered and headed for the front porch. "How did you know that I wasn't at the center anymore, anyway?"

"I went by there today," I stated and followed Arlene inside. "I had something to tell you."

"Well, tell me now."

"I made the team," I announced and grinned, pride all over my face.

"You made the high-school basketball team?"

"Yes, ma'am."

"Tee, you for real?"

"Yes, I'm for real."

"Oh, baby, that's wonderful! I'm so proud of you."

I'd waited my whole life just to hear those words from my mother—that she was proud of me...that I had done a good job. I guess part of me had done this for her, for her approval, her pride, her love. I hoped it would bring her home again.

"My first game is the day after Thanksgiving, and I want you to be there."

"I'm there, baby. You can believe that!" she declared and was genuinely happy for me. I could see it on her face. I could even feel it when she grabbed me in her arms and hugged me tighter than she ever had before. "I'm done with the drugs, Tee. I'm ten days clean, and I won't turn back. I promise."

For some reason, I believed her this time.

I went into the kitchen and popped my pizza into the microwave. Had no idea that the day would turn out this way. Life was pretty good.

twenty-two

Jade

Mattie pushed the basket through the aisles at Publix, nearly knocking boxes off the shelves as she turned the corner. Mommy's attention was on the package of ground beef in her hand as she compared the prices of the other meats.

"Maybe I'll make some spaghetti tonight," she announced. "Jade, run over to the frozen-food section and grab some of that garlic bread that we like so much. Can you do that?"

"Yes, ma'am."

I couldn't understand why we had to make grocery shopping a family affair. Did she really need for Mattie and me to tag along? It seemed senseless to me, but I remained a trooper. As I headed over to the frozen-food section, a package of chips caught my eye along the way and I grabbed them. Figured I would slip them into the basket while Mommy wasn't looking, and then by the time she got halfway through the checkout line it would be too late to put them back. Worked every time. The cold air rushed across my face as I opened the glass door of the freezer and pulled out a box of garlic bread. By the time I made it back to where Mattie and the basket were parked, Mommy was checking the expiration dates on the gallons of milk. I tossed the chips into the basket.

"You can't have those," Mattie said.

"Yes, I can. Shut up."

"I'm telling."

Mommy walked up and placed the milk into the basket. "Telling what?" she asked.

"Jade got chips," she accused and held the bag in the air.

I snatched them from her.

"Mattie, it's not polite to be a tattletale," Mommy said. "Are you just upset because you didn't get any?"

I was shocked by my mother's response. She was on my side for once and I wasn't used to that. I was planning to apologize to her for my behavior the other night, but it was hard. I hadn't been able to find the right words.

"Sorry, Mommy," I just went for it and said. "About the other night and the way I acted..."

She just stared as if she was waiting for more.

"...I wasn't trying to be disrespectful. I just wanted to

get to the pool before my friends left and before it got dark outside. I was gonna do my chores as soon as I came back inside. You just came home early that day."

"Honestly, Jade, you're not being punished because you went to the pool, nor because you failed to do your chores. It was the way you handled it. It was your attitude that sent me through the roof."

"I know," I concurred. I remembered my attitude that night and it wasn't anything nice.

"You know, we all make mistakes and do things that we shouldn't. But we have to be able to handle them the right way. We have to accept responsibility for our actions. That's what it's all about," she explained and placed a dozen eggs into the basket. "You want me to tell you how you *should've* handled that situation?"

Not really, I wanted to say, but I didn't. I just shut my mouth and listened.

"When I started fussing about the clothes and the dishes in the sink, you could've simply said, 'Sorry, Mommy, I wanted to get to the pool before my friends left and before it got dark outside. I'm gonna do my chores right now.' And that would've been the end of it. But instead you started rolling your eyes into the back of your head. I thought you were having a seizure or something..."

Mattie giggled, which caused my mother to giggle, too.

"That attitude of yours is something else, Jade. I laugh because I was the same way when I was your age. Bad

Attitude Barbara, is what they should've called me," she admitted and touched my face with the palm of her hand. "A bad attitude gets you nowhere. You can get so much further if you lose it."

I wasn't expecting a lecture in the middle of the milk aisle at Publix. I just wanted to get something off my chest, so that I could stop carrying around the guilt of it. She had a point about handling things the right way, and I definitely hadn't handled things with Chocolate Boy all that well. He had poured his heart out to me, and admitted things that were hurtful and embarrassing for him, and I pretty much turned my back on him. Just like everyone else in his life had done. I owed him an apology, too.

"I tell you what I'm gonna do, Jade-bug," Mommy continued. "I'm gonna turn your phone back on tonight. I was just waiting for you to apologize."

"Really?" I asked, just to be sure I heard her right.

"Really," she said and then hugged me tight.

Stretched across my bed, I tuned my radio to the Quiet Storm on V-103. Grabbed my cell phone and sent Chocolate Boy a text message.

"what u doing?"

I waited for a response. He usually responded right away, but tonight was different.

"got my phone back." That was my next text. I figured he would be thrilled to hear that.

Again, no response.

I dialed his number.

"Please enjoy the music while your party is located," the woman announced as usual.

Lil Wayne's voice rang in my ear. Only this time it was followed by Terrence's voice saying, "Sorry I missed your call, but I'll hit you back just as soon as I can." *Beep*.

I decided not to leave a message. I had already left two and it was obvious that he was either really busy or really ignoring me. Instead, I dialed my father's phone number and asked him if I could spend the weekend with him. I figured that just in case Terrence called back and still wanted to take me to the movies it would be easier to convince my dad to let me go. Actually, I planned on asking Veronica to ask my dad. By the time I hung up the phone, he was thrilled that I wanted to spend time with him, and talked about all the fun stuff we were going to do. I felt guilty using him like that, but some things weren't personal.

I finished the night with a phone call to Indigo and Tameka on three-way, where I found out that going to a movie with Terrence was out of the question. He and Marcus had planned on spending the weekend at Morehouse, on campus, with Tameka's boyfriend, Brian. They were planning to attend a frat party on Friday night, where there would be college-age girls all up in their faces.

"I'm not worried about Marcus," Indigo said. "We have a commitment and we trust each other."

"What about you, Jade? You worried about Terrence?" Tameka asked.

"Nah. Not really," I lied. The truth was, I was very worried. I wasn't even sure if Terrence was still my boyfriend. After the way I treated him, I couldn't blame him if he never spoke to me again. And the thought of him meeting someone new had me shaking in my boots. Terrence was way more mature than your average high-school guy, and maybe what he needed was an older woman, anyway. "Well, I gotta go, y'all. My mama just gave me my phone back. I don't want her taking it again."

"Cool. I'll see you at school in the morning," Indigo said.

"Let's go to the mall on Saturday," Tameka suggested.

"That's cool. Victoria's Secret is having their semi-annual sale," Indigo said. "And Nine West got these boots that I want for Christmas."

"Oh, yeah, Christmas! I need to start getting my list together," Tameka exclaimed. "Are you in for Saturday, Jade?"

"Yeah, I'm in. I'm supposed to spend the weekend with my dad and his girlfriend, but I'll ask if I can go to the mall on Saturday."

"Cool. I gotta go. 'Flavor of Love' is about to come on," Tameka announced.

"Me, too. I got dishes to load into the dishwasher before calling Marcus," Indigo said.

Before I could say that I was just going to finish listening to the Quiet Storm, both of them had hung up. I stayed awake for another thirty minutes, hoping that Terrence would return my call. He didn't.

twenty-three

Terrence

Brian whipped his little Nissan Sentra into the parking lot at the Atlanta University Center. The bass from his stereo had pounded in my ears throughout the entire drive to the West End.

"Here we are, brothers. You can leave your bags in the trunk for now and we'll get them later."

Marcus and I stepped out of the car. People were gathered near "the stoop" as Brian referred to it. It was an area where everybody hung out, chitchatted about important or unimportant things, and caught up on what was happening on campus.

"This here is my frat brother, Key. We call him Key because he's a master on the keyboards," Brian said, referring to a tall, slender dude who wore his hair in dreadlocks. He wore flip-flops, a pair of shorts and a pullover hoodie. "This is Marcus Carter and Terrence Hill. They're considering a college career here."

"Just considering," Marcus said and then shook Key's hand.

"Glad to meet you," I said and did the same.

"Oh, yeah, this young brother has his heart set on one of them Ivy League schools. But I promise by the end of this weekend, he'll be asking for an application."

"No doubt," Key chimed in. "Y'all going to the frat party tonight?"

"We is there," Brian said in bad English and then gave his frat brother a handshake.

The three of us began a tour of the campus.

"Over here is a little café where students hang out, do homework or whatever. Some of the girls from Spelman come over here and hang out sometimes. A lot of the students from Clark come over, too."

Two beautiful girls stood outside a place called Jazzman's Café chitchatting and sipping on something hot, like coffee or hot chocolate. They grinned as we walked past, and Marcus and I grinned back, thinking they were looking at us.

"Hey, Brian," they sang in unison.

"How you doing, ladies?" he asked.

"Good," one of them answered.

"How did you do on your physics exam?" the other one asked.

"B+," he boasted. "Thanks for all your help, Belinda."

"Anytime," Belinda answered and smiled his way and I wondered what type of help she had really given him.

"A pretty tutor never hurt anybody," he whispered to us as we took the corner near a huge antique-looking bell. "This is Sale Hall, and that's the historic Chapel Bell. That's where you take your religion and philosophy classes. They also have a small auditorium inside where they have recitals and stuff like that..."

It was fascinating walking in between the buildings and walking where famous black men had also walked.

"It's nothing for Spike Lee or Jesse Jackson, or even Bill Cosby to be seen walking these very campus grounds. Nobody even makes a fuss, it's just the norm," Brian said. "Now come on, let me show you the King Chapel and the statue of Dr. Martin Luther King, Jr."

In the base of the statue you could read the words of Dr. King. It almost felt as if his spirit was still there, roaming the campus, watching over us.

"I didn't even know that Dr. King went to Morehouse before the other day," I had to admit.

"He was definitely a Morehouse man, got his sociology degree from here in 1948."

As we approached a statue named Thurman Obelisk, a bell started chiming.

"This is where Dr. Thurman and his wife's ashes are."

"Who's Dr. Thurman?"

"He was a great preacher, who Dr. King patterned

himself after," Brian explained. "He wrote a book called *The Inward Journey.* You heard of it?"

"Not me," I admitted.

"Me, either," Marcus said. "What's that tune that I'm hearing?"

"The bell chimes every hour to Morehouse's alma mater, 'Dear Old Morehouse.'"

"How do you remember so much of the history here?" Marcus asked. "Are you a history major or something?"

"Not at all. In your freshman year on campus, you take a class where they teach you about your heritage and the history of Morehouse. You might think, 'Aw, I don't want to take a class like that and learn some boring history.' But it's really not like that. It's really enlightening."

"That's cool," I decided and smiled, fascinated by everything around me. At that moment, I knew there was no doubt that I would become a Morehouse man.

When we walked into the frat party, several brothers were onstage dressed in matching black T-shirts and black Timberland boots. The crowd was going crazy as they bounced around, stepping and chanting. The way they were stepping in unison made me wish I was up there, too. The place was packed and you could barely move around. Girls were smiling and flirting with their eyes, and I wondered if they knew that Marcus and I were high-school kids. We didn't care, the attention was mind-blowing.

A girl with long, silky hair, wearing tight jeans and a tight shirt that barely covered her shoulders, brushed past me carrying a wine cooler. Her hand caressed my chest as she walked past and winked. I smiled.

"You see that, man?" I asked Marcus. I didn't want to sound juvenile, but I couldn't help it. It wasn't every day that beautiful girls flirted so blatantly. As a matter of fact, the girls I went to high school with weren't that bold at all. They played silly little games when they were interested in you. They would never touch you like that—not intentionally.

"Check out the honey over here in the red. She checkin' me out, while I'm checkin' her out," Marcus said.

"This weekend, brothers, you are single Morehouse men with no girlfriends at home," Brian whispered. "Now go on over there and say hi to the ladies."

In my opinion, I no longer had a girlfriend. Jade had pretty much made her judgment about me and decided I wasn't good enough for her. I couldn't blame her. My life was filled with more drama than a soap opera. I couldn't expect her to stick around for that. I thought she was my friend though, but when she started dodging me at school and not returning my calls, it was clear that she really wasn't. I saw her name on my call log, but by that time, I'd already written her off. I didn't have time for games—and as it seemed, I really didn't have time for a girlfriend, anyway.

I walked over to the girl who had just given my chest a rubdown. Her seductive eyes followed me the whole way.

"How you doing? I'm Terrence," I asserted. I wasn't shy.

"Jennifer," she replied and held her hand out to me. "Nice to meet you, Terrence. You attend Morehouse?"

"Not yet, but I'm considering it. Especially now." I found myself flirting with the girl who I hadn't even noticed had hazel-colored eyes and a dimple on the right side of her face. Her body had more curves than the women I saw in the videos on BET.

As the step team finished their routine, Flo Rida's voice shook the room.

"You wanna dance?"

"Yeah," I said and followed Jennifer to the dance floor.

She grabbed my hand as the bangles on her wrist played a tune. She didn't waste any time moving her hips to the music, and I followed her lead. I moved to the music, while trying to keep my cool, but it was hard. I looked over at Marcus who was dancing with the girl in red. He started cheesing and I did the same. He seemed too cozy with a girl he'd just met and I wondered if Indigo would be smiling if she was watching.

Jennifer and I ended up outside in Atlanta's cool night air. I unzipped my jacket and placed it around her shoulders.

"Ah, you're a gentleman, too," she said.

"Yes, I am," I agreed and laughed when there was nothing really funny. My nervous energy was getting the best of me. "Where do you go to school?"

"Clark Atlanta," she said. "Sophomore."

I was a junior, just not in college. I was hoping she didn't ask me what grade I was in. Hoped that she just assumed I was a senior. Being a senior seemed closer to adulthood. I changed the subject before she had a chance to ask.

"What's your major?" I asked her.

"I haven't really decided on one yet. I'm still just kind of finding my way through college. My daddy wants me to go to medical school and become a doctor like him. But I'm more of an arts person, and would love to do something with my photography."

So her father was a doctor. This girl was way out of my league and I knew it, but she was beautiful…and interesting. And we were just having a conversation.

"So you're thinking about becoming a Morehouse man, huh?"

"Yeah, I think so. I hadn't really considered college at all until now," I continued and just laid it on the table. I had learned my lesson about keeping things inside. "I honestly never thought that college was a real possibility for me, until now."

"Why now?"

"Just visiting the Morehouse campus has changed my way of thinking."

"You're still in high school?"

"Yeah," I answered honestly.

"What grade?"

"Eleventh," I answered. I didn't care what she thought at this point. If she wanted to walk away, it was nothing new. I was used to people doing that.

"Wow, you seem so much older. You're really mature," she proclaimed and smiled. "Unlike some college guys that I know. They all have one-track minds—sex on the brain. But you seem different, Terrence. And your eyes...they're so mysterious. Why?"

"I don't know why. I have a lot going on in my life, a lot of things that I hide from the rest of the world."

"Like what?"

"You don't wanna hear my problems," I declared and laughed nervously, hoping she would change the subject and we could move on to a more comfortable conversation.

"I do. Tell me. Tell me why there's so much mystery in your eyes, Terrence."

"Let's just say that I had to become a man much sooner than I really wanted to," I admitted. Didn't want to put my mother's dirty laundry in the streets, but it felt good to express that—even to a stranger. "My mother had some things going on in her life, that left me with a lot of responsibility."

"Same here," she said. "When I was twelve years old, my mother became strung out on drugs and walked out on my father. He was left to raise three little girls all by himself. And since I was the oldest of those three little girls, I had to help Daddy take care of my little sisters."

"Wow, are you for real?" I asked.

"Yep," she said. "And you know the funny thing about it is...we've all done very well. I'm a sophomore in college. One of my sisters is at Spelman. She's a freshman this year.

And my baby sister will probably get a full scholarship to go somewhere. She's not sure where she's going yet, but she's an honor student. So they'll be throwing money her way."

"Now, that's cool right there." All I kept thinking was how easy Jennifer was to talk to. "My mother was kinda out there on drugs, too. But she's getting it together now."

"That's good." She smiled. "My mother has since come back. She wants to be a part of our lives now, after my father did all the work. My two little sisters have let her back in, but I guess I'm the stubborn one. I'm not so forgiving because I've seen too much."

"You know, you have to forgive her though. She probably didn't mean to hurt you," I told her.

I thought about Arlene. She had hurt me, too, but I knew she didn't mean to. It was just one of those things. She was trapped and really didn't know a way out. But I think she found her way, and I was glad for that.

"I know I have to forgive her, but only in my own time," Jennifer said.

I loved her honesty, and the way she just opened up to me.

"What made you tell me all that, Jennifer? You don't know me from Adam, and that was a lot of information we just shared."

"I don't know. You seem so genuine, Terrence. From the moment I asked your name," she said, "I knew you were different. And I'll tell you something else..."

"What's that?"

"I'm glad you're considering college now. It's not even

an option for kids like us. We have to beat the odds. Show the world what we're made of, despite our past," she said. "And I know where to find all the scholarship money. So when you're ready, you let me know and I'll help you get money for school."

"For real? It's that simple?"

"It's that simple," she announced and sounded like an authority on the matter. "Wanna go inside? It's just a little too chilly out here for me."

"Yeah, we can go in."

She started walking toward the door and I grabbed her small hand in mine.

"Thank you," I said.

"For what?" she asked.

"For allowing me to be myself."

She dug into her purse, found a pen. She grabbed my hand and turned it palm side up. She wrote her phone number in the palm of my hand and then stuck the pen back into her purse. She kissed my cheek and then said, "Call me sometime."

Before I knew it she had vanished into the crowd of people, and I wondered if she had been just a dream. If so, I was not ready to wake up.

twenty-four

Jade

The mall was as crowded as it usually was on a Saturday afternoon. It seemed that everybody from my school and their mamas was there. We checked out Victoria's Secret's semiannual sale, and I ended up with some new underwear. Daddy had given me thirty dollars to spend, and I thought I would use it for something worthwhile. Mommy usually picked out my underwear and I thought it was time to give the bloomers a rest. Instead, I'd found some boy-cut panties in loud colors like lime green and bright orange, and even a pair of hot-pink ones. After my underwear purchase, I had just enough money left for the food court.

At Chik-fil-A, I ordered my favorite—chicken tenders with a small order of waffle fries, and a large Coke. Indigo had found us a table in the middle of the food court and was waving as she saw me walking past. Tameka set her Lady Foot Locker bag and her new Coach purse on the empty seat between us.

"I just talked to Brian. Your men are having the time of their lives," she said.

"Marcus told me they went to a party last night," Indigo added. "And they're going to another one tonight."

"We should crash the party," Tameka suggested.

"I trust Marcus completely. I'm not interested in checking up on him," said Indigo. "I wouldn't want him doing that to me."

"What about you, Miss Thing? You haven't mentioned Terrence's name once this weekend."

"There's nothing to say," I responded.

"Aren't you just a little bit curious about what your boyfriend is doing on campus?" Tameka asked.

"He's not really my boyfriend…anymore."

"Y'all broke up?" Indi asked. She was surprised that I hadn't shared the latest news with her, when we shared just about everything.

"Something like that."

"What do you mean 'something like that'?"

"He tried to open up to me about some stuff, and I turned my back on him. End of story."

"You talking about the rumor that Felicia Clark was spreading? I told you to consider the source," Indigo said. "That girl is stupid. I don't even know why you hang out with her."

"I don't really hang out with her. I just talk to her sometimes."

"Maybe you can talk to Terrence. Tell him you're sorry or something," Indi suggested.

"He hates me now," I said. "He's probably already moved on."

"There's only one way to find out. We're going to that party!" Tameka announced. "Are y'all in or what?"

"In," Indigo said.

"I guess I'm in, too," I said.

It wasn't hard to convince Daddy to let me spend the night at Tameka's house. My parents had already met Tameka's parents and had respect for them, so spending the night was never a problem. Mel baked us homemade deep-dish pizza in the oven—loaded with Italian sausage and mushrooms—and we ate like there was no tomorrow. After dinner, the three of us lounged in the backyard, sipping peach iced tea and flipped through old *Vibe* magazines. Tameka was looking for a new hairstyle and she thought she might find one in there.

"Meagan Good's hair is cute in this photo," I said and held up my issue of *Vibe* and showed her the picture.

"How about this one?" Tameka asked, holding up a photo of Mariah Carey. "I like that color, too."

"You planning on coloring your hair, too?" Indigo asked.

"I don't know. I might."

"You should just do some highlights," I suggested. "That would be cute."

"Maybe you could just go natural like your girl, Erykah Badu," Indigo said and smiled and showed us her issue of *Vibe* where Erykah was sporting a nappy brown afro.

We all laughed, and I tried to imagine Tameka with a nappy brown afro, holding an afro pick to fork it out.

"No, thanks," Tameka protested and grinned.

"What you wearing to the party tonight?" Indigo asked Tameka.

"My new Apple Bottoms, of course," Tameka said. "What about y'all?"

"I'm wearing the jeans I bought at the mall, and my cute little top from the Papaya store," Indigo said.

"I brought my Seven jeans and my red boots," I offered and flipped through the *Vibe* magazine and saw an article about Beyoncé. "I got two red tops and I need to decide which one to wear."

"Well, let's go inside and see what they look like," Tameka insisted and hopped off her lawn chair. We followed her upstairs to her room.

"How are we getting to the party, by the way?" I had to ask, because no one seemed to be discussing that small detail.

Tameka dangled a set of keys from her fingertips. "I got the keys to Benz-o!"

"For real? Mel's letting you drive her car?" Indigo asked.

"Of course. I got my driver's license," she boasted. "But this is the first time she let me get the wheels by myself."

"Your mama is so cool!" I said. "I gotta hurry up and get my license. I got my permit, but that's about it. But I bet my daddy would let me get his car."

"You need to put that on your list of things to do before the school year ends," Tameka said. "My dad's buying me a car for my birthday in March. I'll be driving to school next year."

"I'm definitely putting it on my to-do list," Indigo proclaimed and started pulling clothes out of her overnight bag and laying them on Tameka's bed. "How 'bout this top with my jeans?"

"That's cute, but I got a top that would go perfect with your jeans. It matches your stitching and everything."

"What shoes you planning on wearing, Indi?" I asked.

"My brown Chuck Taylors if I wear the brown top," she said.

"Don't forget that this is a college party," Tameka reminded us. "We have to look the part."

"I don't think college kids are that much into fashion. And besides, my Chucks are all that," Indi said. "I'm wearing 'em. And I'm first in the shower."

The wheels on Mel's champagne-colored Benz scraped the curb as Tameka parallel parked it into a tight spot in Atlanta's West End. The music was loud enough to be heard outside, and people were standing in line to get inside. The three of us got in line behind two guys wearing T-shirts with Greek writing across the front. They were obviously fraternity brothers. One of them smiled at Indigo as she nervously zipped her leather jacket all the way up. He continued to flirt with his eyes as his friend checked me out.

"Y'all go to Spelman?" one of them asked.

Indigo shook her head no, and we were grateful when the line started moving and we reached the front. We were shocked when the lady behind the wooden counter asked us for ten dollars each. Indigo dug into her purse and pulled out a crumpled five-dollar bill. And I knew there was no need in me opening my purse, because the most I had was two dollars and a Dave & Buster's token.

"I got it," Tameka said and pulled two twenty-dollar bills out of her purse, handed it to the lady, who was looking as if she was about to have us thrown out.

We slowly walked in and squeezed our way to the side of the room where we found a small corner to stand in. The music was so loud that you could literally feel the bass pounding in your chest. There was no room on the dance floor to walk, much less dance. People were packed in like sardines. I immediately spotted Marcus on the dance floor and nudged Indigo to look his way.

"I wonder if he saw me," she said.

"Probably not," I said. He was too busy dancing to see anybody.

"I'm going over there," she said.

"No!" Tameka said. "We have to be cool. You can't

run over there acting like a high-school girl, Indigo. He's just dancing."

"I don't think that Brian's just dancing," I said as I spotted Tameka's boyfriend in a dark corner with some girl. "He's over there in the corner."

I tried to whisper it to Indigo, but Tameka overheard me and zoomed in on him. I could almost see the smoke escaping from her ears. She was furious, and rightly so. His lips were locked with another girl's and he held on to her as if she belonged right there in his arms.

"I'm going over there," she said.

"You can't," I said. "You just told us that we have to be cool…that we can't act like high-school girls."

"Forget that!" Tameka yelled. "This is different. His lips are all locked with some other hoochie! I can't just stand by and watch."

Tears filled her eyes, and my heart reached out to her.

"You should wait until you get yourself together, Tameka, before going over there," I suggested. I grabbed her hand in mine, and hoped that would make her feel better. Indigo grabbed her other hand and we stood there for a moment wondering what to do.

"Let's just go, Tameka," Indigo said. "He's not even worth the confrontation."

"I gotta let him know that I saw him," she said and sniffed. "I can't believe he was just on the phone with me last night…talking about how much he love me, and telling me that I'm the only girl for him…"

"We should just go. You can call him on the phone tonight and tell him," I said.

Tameka contemplated what her next action would be. I could feel someone across the room staring my way. When I turned to look in that direction, my eyes locked with Terrence's. He gave me a smile and then headed my way.

"What you doing here?" he whispered in my ear.

"Looking for you," I admitted. It was the truth.

"Well, here I am," he said. "You wanna dance?"

A slow Chris Brown tune filled the room, and Terrence's hand grabbed mine as he led me to the crowded dance floor. He pulled me close to him as we slow danced.

"I'm sorry about the other day," I said, "I didn't mean to run away like that."

"It's cool."

"I missed you," I uttered and was trying to get as much conversation in as possible, hoping for his forgiveness.

"Missed you, too," he said. "I'm glad to see you, Morgan."

As my head rested against his chest, I knew that we would be all right. I thought the same thing about Marcus and Indigo as they had found each other in the midst of the crowd and held on to each other on the dance floor just a few feet away. But as I watched Tameka yelling at Brian, one hand on her hip, a finger pointed in his face and her neck rolling from side to side, I knew their relationship had reached its unhappily ever after.

twenty-five

Terrence

I stood at the free-throw line, dressed in metallic red shorts and a matching jersey, *HILL* plastered across the back of it in bold white letters and the number 23 in the center of my back—the same number as LeBron James and Michael Jordan, my favorite two players in the NBA. I bounced the ball twice and then tossed it into the hoop. Missed.

"Take your time, Hill," I heard Coach yell across the gym.

I bounced the ball again, looked up at the goal. Bounced some more, and then tossed the ball into the hoop for a second time. It went in with a swishing noise and the crowd cheered. Three of my teammates went for the rebound, and somebody from the other team took it downcourt. Marcus gave me a high five as we rushed down court to play defense.

The game had been a good one. We were leading by six

points, which was better than we'd done in the first quarter. In the first quarter it seemed impossible for us to even take possession of the ball, but now with just two minutes left on the clock in the second quarter, we were feeling pretty confident about the game. Alfredo, our six-foot Hispanic center, went up for a block, slapping the ball toward me. I took off downcourt with it. It seemed I had the entire court to myself as I dunked the ball—a trick I'd learned in the seventh grade on the rusty goal at the end of my block. The crowd went crazy. The shot put us up by eight points, and I hoped we would win our first game of the season.

At halftime, a Jay-Z tune rang out through the gym, and the dance team rushed out to the center of the floor dressed in little pleated red shorts and tight red tops. They started moving their hips in unison and I zeroed in on Jade. She and Indigo were shaking harder than any of the other girls. It was obvious they were the best dancers in the group as they bounced to the music.

While the dance team shook their hips like crazy, I scanned the bleachers. Sydney was waving at me and Trey was giving me a thumbs-up. Arlene was seated in between them, grinning from ear to ear. Not only had she kept her promise of showing up at my first game, but she'd kept her promise of staying drug-free. And for that, I was proud of her. She spent each day combing Syd's hair and helping Trey with his math—as best she could. She admitted that she wasn't that good in math when she was younger, but she did her best. And she was there for them when they rushed in from the bus stop every afternoon, freeing me up to go to basketball practice. In the late evenings she attended her AA meetings downtown every day. I could see a definite change in her, and I was grateful to God for answering my prayers. I used to wonder if he even heard me when I prayed, but this time he did.

Aunt Brenda had stopped coming around so much, and I wondered what was happening to their friendship. I guess the change in Arlene was too much for Aunt Brenda to handle, so she probably found other friends. Sometimes doing the right thing left you a little lonely, but maybe Arlene would find new friends—friends who had been through similar things and wanted to change their lives. Friends who would encourage her to stay on the right path. That's what I wished for her. She had her face made up with lipstick, eye shadow and everything. She'd even been taking better care of her hair. When she blew me a kiss, I blew her one back.

After the dance team's routine, the referee blew the whistle to alert us that it was time for the second half of the game to begin. Marcus and I were amongst the five players who took our places on the court. It was the other team's ball, and someone took it out. We played serious defense as they brought the ball downcourt.

Arlene insisted that we go to Church's Chicken to celebrate my team's victory.

"I know it's not Applebee's or nothing like that, but it's what I can afford," she said as she pulled her new Ford Tempo into the parking space in front of Church's.

The Ford Tempo was a gift from Big Tony. He'd fixed the engine, repaired the brakes and put new tires on it, after which it ran like a charm. Big Tony was always doing something good for my family and I kept trying to think of a way of repaying him. Christmas was just around the corner and I was constantly picking his brain about what he might want as a gift. He seemed to have everything—everything except for a family. It had to be lonely for him, being alone like that all the time and never knowing what it meant to belong somewhere, to know the true meaning of family. I was only beginning to understand myself. I knew that Sydney, Trey and I were family, but Arlene never fit into our threesome until now. And I was happy to let her in. But I wanted to give Big Tony that same gift, one way or another.

I remembered the conversation we'd once had about his ex-wife and how she'd run away with his kids, and they never knew that he loved them. His kids were grown now with their own children, and he'd never even met his grandchildren. That seemed like a tragedy in and of itself. What if they wanted to see him and didn't know how to find him? What if they knew where he was, but didn't know how to approach him? Maybe they wanted to be a part of his life, too.

"I wish I could find Big Tony's kids," I told Arlene after we'd ordered and found a booth in the corner of the restaurant.

"What do you mean, 'find his kids,' Terrence?" she asked. "Are they lost?"

"He hasn't seen them since his ex-wife ran off with them when they were little kids," I explained. "He sent letters and cards and she sent them all back. Then pretty soon, he just lost contact altogether."

"What does that have to do with you, Tee?"

"I wish I could find them for him, hook 'em up so they could spend Christmas together," I explained. "Do you know what Big Tony did last Christmas?"

"No, what?"

"He spent the whole day putting a new engine into a truck," I said.

"Maybe that's what he wanted to do, Tee," she said. "And besides, you can't just go around finding people's kids. He might not want to see them. Or vice versa, they might not want to see him."

"Well, I know he wants to see them," I announced and bit into my chicken leg. "And what kid wouldn't want to see their parent? It seems like they would be curious about him. He's a real cool dude. Who wouldn't want to hang out with him?"

"I think you're living in a fantasy world, baby. People are different in real life. That kinda stuff only happens on TV," Arlene said and stole one of Trey's French fries when he looked away.

"Well, can we at least invite him to spend Christmas with us this year...so he doesn't have to be alone?"

"I don't see anything wrong with that. He's done so much for us, I think it would be nice to invite him over," she said. "Are we having dinner or something? While you're making all these plans, you must be cooking."

"We can do that," I agreed but hadn't thought of that before now, and I had gotten to be a pretty good cook. "I can fry some chicken, Aunt Brenda can do her famous potato salad..."

"I love Aunt Brenda's potato salad!" Sydney exclaimed. "It's so good."

"You can fix your homemade rolls," I told Arlene.

"Boy, I haven't done homemade rolls in a minute."

"I was seven the last time you did them," I reminded her.

"And you remember that?"

"Yes, I do," I attested and smiled. "Will you do them?"

"I'll see if I can find your grandmother's old recipe. Boy, you gon' make me pull out some skills I ain't used in a long time," she said. "Pulling out old recipes is like pulling old skeletons out of the closet."

It was no secret that Arlene and her mother didn't get along. When Arlene got pregnant with me and started living the street life, my grandmother pretty much shut her out. They fought and argued right up until the day that Grandmother passed away. Arlene never forgave herself for not being around to say goodbye. And she was too torn up to attend the funeral. They never had a chance to put the past behind them and just be family.

"Sometimes it's good to pull skeletons out of the closet,"

I assured her and smiled. "You know Grandmother loved you, even though she didn't know how to show it."

It was sort of like that with me and Arlene. She loved us, but sometimes she really didn't know how to show it. She made us call her Arlene because she wasn't quite sure how to be our mother. But I believed that all of that would change for her. I knew she loved us, even though she didn't hug me much, didn't kiss me much. I could hear it in her voice when she announced that she was going to rehab. And I could see it in her smile when she met Jade, and when she blew me a kiss from the bleachers at the basketball game. There was definitely love in her eyes as we sat in that little booth at Church's Chicken, eating a meal that I knew she couldn't really afford.

"When did you get to be so smart, Tee?" she asked. "You really did grow up before my eyes. I missed so much with you."

"You haven't missed much. I'm still the same old Tee," I said.

"If you want me to make the homemade rolls, then I will. But it's up to you to find the recipe. I don't know what I did with it."

"I already found it," I confessed and grinned. "It's in the kitchen drawer at home."

"You a mess," she said.

I couldn't remember the last time I'd been as happy as I was at that moment.

versations with my own Chinese comments. That would be hilarious.

I peeked over to my left as Mattie got her nails painted hot pink to match her toes. She grinned when I looked her way.

"Look at my design, Jade," she said and showed me the flower on her middle fingernail, surrounded by fake rhinestones.

"That's cute."

"You should get a design, too," she said too loud.

"Use your inside voice, Mattie," I reminded her.

She whispered, "You should get a design, too."

"Get whatever you want, girls," Veronica said. "Jade, this is your day to be pampered."

She was right about that. Birthdays only came once a year and they didn't last long when they showed up, either. My only regret was that my birthday fell a week before Christmas, which meant that I usually got short-cutted on the gifts. My parents always either gave me my Christmas gifts on my birthday, or my birthday gifts on Christmas—and either way the math didn't add up. I should've been able to request something big at least twice a year, but it didn't work that way. Whatever expensive thing I wanted, I got either for my birthday or Christmas. Never both.

"You know, Jade, just because your birthday is right before Christmas, doesn't mean they have to be celebrated together," Veronica said as if she had read my

twenty-six

Jade

The Asian woman who filed my nails and rounded them off in the corners smiled as I leaned back in her chair. She started speaking in Chinese to the woman who was pressing acrylic tips onto Veronica's nails, and I wondered if they were talking about us. I always wondered if Asian people were talking about us when they spoke in their native language at the nail shop where we got our nails done, or at the beauty supply stores where Mommy picked up Mattie's *Just For Me* hair kit, or when we visited our favorite Chinese buffet. They always seemed to look our way when they spoke, and sometimes they even had little smirks in the corners of their mouths. I made it my goal to take a Chinese class when I got older, just so I could understand what was being said. I often wondered how they would react if I interrupted their con-

mind. "Tell me one big thing you want for your birthday, and then tell me one big thing you want for Christmas."

I had to think about it. I had one big thing in mind, because that was usually how it went. I knew that I wanted a stereo to replace the clock radio that I listened to the Quiet Storm on. There were several little things on my wish list, like an Apple iPod, my own laptop computer so that I wouldn't have to share one with Mommy and Mattie, and I wanted some new clothes that I could pick out myself. I saw a pair of boots at Macy's that I wanted, and a silver necklace at Parisian.

But what I wanted more than anything in the whole world was for Terrence to treat me the way he did before his visit to Morehouse. Something about him changed in that weekend. Something changed between us, and I couldn't quite put my finger on it. It wasn't that he treated me bad, but the sparkle in his eye wasn't there anymore, and I wondered why. He was harder to reach by phone, and he only returned my text messages at his convenience. I felt as if I was losing him. When I asked him about it, he said that my imagination was getting the best of me.

Something was definitely different.

I looked over at Veronica, and remembered how I had judged her. I had wished bad things for her—like getting hit by a truck or falling from the ninth floor of her office building. I hated the fact that she was stealing my family away—or so I thought. My family had already fallen apart and I didn't know it. So instead of embracing her, I hated her instead. I had judged her just like I had judged Terrence when he told me about his mother. And because of it I had lost my boyfriend. He was still around, but a piece of him was missing.

So if she really wanted to know what big things I wanted for my birthday and Christmas, it would be a stereo—and the chance to win back the heart of Chocolate Boy.

"A stereo for my room," I said.

"Okay, that's easy enough. I'll discuss that with your parents," she said.

"And the second thing...it's kind of stupid..."

Boy troubles were never things that I could discuss with either of my parents. Daddy was not trying to hear anything about a boy. In his mind, he was the only man in my life. And Mommy; she thought that my focus should be on school—and that's it. No social life unless it was for the benefit of my future. That was probably why my daddy's and her marriage didn't last. She was too serious all the time. She didn't know how to let her hair down and just have fun. Daddy needed to laugh, and Mommy probably wouldn't let him. Their differences probably ruined their marriage.

But the one thing they saw eye to eye on was Mattie and me. They were a team when it came to raising us, even while living in separate apartments. Whenever I did something wrong, Mommy was on the phone with Daddy in an instant. And before he could ever make a decision about me, he called her to get her opinion. There was no pulling either of their strings. They were too close.

"I wouldn't think it was stupid," Veronica offered and smiled. "Try me. I've been through just about everything you're going through right now. I survived my parents' divorce, and I hated my new stepmother, too…for a while. Until I got to know her, and discovered that she was a wonderful lady who did a fantastic job raising me after my mother passed away."

"Your mom passed away?"

"When I was fifteen," she said.

"I'm sorry," I said.

"Thank you, Jade. I just want you to know that you're not alone in this world," she said. "Now, what other big thing do you want for Christmas?"

"Well, there's this boy that I like. His name is Terrence…"

"The cute one that you went to the homecoming dance with," she observed and smiled. "He was fine."

I blushed.

"Yeah, that's him. We been going out since last school year, and I thought that he really liked me, until…"

"Until?"

"Well, these girls that live in my apartment complex. They're always gossiping and spreading rumors about people. And they told me that Terrence's mama was strung out on drugs and that he used drugs and sold them, too."

"Did you ask him about it?"

"Yeah. And the only part that was true was that his mama

was strung out on drugs. And the reason why he worked so much and never asked me out on dates was because he was busy taking care of his little brother and sister."

"Wow, that's very admirable," Veronica admitted and smiled. "I like him already."

"It scared me a little—having a boyfriend whose mama was strung out on drugs. I was embarrassed about what my friends might think if they found out. I thought they would judge me and treat me like an outcast..."

"Well, that's where you went wrong...it wasn't even about you," she said. "It was about him. And it probably took everything he had inside him just to share that with you."

"I know that now, and I apologized for the way I reacted."

"Did he accept your apology?"

"Yes, but things are different now. I'm still his girlfriend, I think. But he doesn't treat me the same. I think I messed up."

"Hmm. This is a tough one," Veronica said, as the Asian woman filled her nails with acrylic.

"Well, that's the one big thing I want for Christmas...for Terrence to treat me the way that he used to...for that sparkle to come back into his eyes."

"I know you probably think he's the only boy in the world right now, but you're still young, sweetie, and there will be so many more with that same sparkle in their eyes. You can't wish for someone's feelings to change. He sounds like a really great guy, Jade, and if he's the one, that's nice. But if he's not, then it's okay. Sometimes people come into our lives for just a moment to teach us things."

"What do you mean?"

"Well, did you learn anything from the way you treated Terrence?"

"Yeah, I learned that you shouldn't judge people."

"There you go," she said. "Do you enjoy spending time with him? And did he treat you like a friend?"

"Yes."

"Then it was time well spent. Think of it like that."

It was easy for her to say. Chocolate Boy was my first real boyfriend, and there were no guarantees that there would be that many more with sparkles in their eyes. I wasn't the prettiest girl in the world, not like Indigo who could have any boy she wanted. And my body was still awkward, unlike Tameka who had curves like her mother, Mel. Boys loved girls with curves. Chocolate Boy had liked me for me.

"You have a lot to offer, Jade. You're beautiful, smart…you have parents who love you to death, which means you come from a good home, with a good upbringing. You're outgoing. You're a great dancer," she insisted and smiled. "As soon as you adjust your attitude just a little bit…you'll have boys knocking each other over just to get to you."

I smiled.

"And all is not lost with Terrence. He might just need some time. He's got a lot on his plate right now. Too much for a boy his age, in my opinion, but a lot, no less," she said. "Just try to be there for him. Be a friend to him and encourage him."

"His mom is doing much better. She went to rehab, and she's been clean for almost two months. And Terrence was able to go out for basketball. He actually made the team, and he's starting, too!"

"It sounds like you're happy for him, and you're proud of him. You should tell him that."

"I should...shouldn't I?"

"Yes, you should!" she assured her and laughed. "I tell you what. We're having Christmas dinner at my house in Powder Springs. How would you like to invite Terrence and his family to spend Christmas with us?"

"Daddy would never go for that."

"You let me handle your father. There's plenty of room for everyone. I've even invited your mom to come. She's making her famous corn-bread dressing."

"Really...Mommy's coming, too?"

"Yep, she is. And your father has already invited Indigo and her parents. Even Marcus and his parents are coming," she added and sounded excited. "And if you want to, you can invite your friend Tameka and her parents, too."

"It would probably just be Tameka and her mom. Her dad is never around."

"What do you think about inviting Terrence and his family? Are you okay with that?"

"Yeah, that would be cool."

"Okay, well, let's make it happen."

Veronica was all right.

The birthday cake was covered in cream-cheese icing and had sixteen candles burning on top. Mattie, Mommy, Daddy, Veronica, Indigo and Tameka all sang six different versions of "Happy Birthday" to me off-key. After blowing out the candles, I couldn't wait to rip the paper from the wrapped gifts that were stacked on Daddy's dining-room table. I decided to go for the biggest one first, even though good things came in small packages. It was a good thing I chose the big one, because inside was the stereo that I'd been asking for all year. No more listening to V-103's Quiet Storm on the little clock radio next to my bed. I had a real stereo, with a real CD player and life would be different.

After opening the rest of my gifts—a DKNY sweat suit from Macy's, a pair of chocolate-brown Nike shoes, a pair of sleep pants from Victoria's Secret and a Mary J. Blige CD—I was anxious to get to the movie theater with Indi and Tameka. There wasn't much playing at the movies, but I just wanted to get out of the house and celebrate my birthday with my friends.

As the three of us piled into Mel's Mercedes and popped in my Mary J. CD, I knew that my sixteenth birthday might turn out all right.

twenty-seven

Terrence

I flipped through the white pages, scrolled through the list of names before finally settling in on the Millers. There were so many of them and I really didn't know where to begin. There was every name from Alfred Miller to Zoe Miller, and every person in between. I knew that Big Tony's son was a junior and began searching for Anthony Miller, Jr. Once I located the long list of Anthony Millers, I flipped open my phone and began calling each of them—one by one.

"Hello, I'm trying to reach Anthony Miller, Jr.," I said to the eleventh one.

"This is Anthony."

"Is your father Anthony Miller who owns Big Tony's Automotive Shop in College Park?"

"No, I'm sorry, you have the wrong number," the man said.

I knew it was probably the wrong number, but there was no harm in trying. I dialed the twelfth number on the list and went through the same routine.

"Is your father Anthony Miller who owns Big Tony's Automotive Shop in College Park?"

"Who's calling please?" the voice on the other end asked.

"I'm Terrence Hill and I work at Big Tony's," I explained. "Are you his son?"

"Why? Did he die or something?" he asked sarcastically.

"No, he's not dead," I said.

"Is he sick?"

"No, he's not sick either," I explained. "I was just trying to locate his children. Because Christmas is just around the corner and..."

"I haven't seen my father since I was a child. What could he possibly want from me for Christmas?"

"He wants to see you."

"Did he say that?" Anthony Jr. asked. "Did he put you up to calling? If so, you can tell my father that I don't have any money to give him."

"He's not interested in your money, man. He just wants to see his children and grandchildren for Christmas."

"I don't think that's possible."

"Why?" I didn't quite understand. How hard would it be to drop by and see your father for Christmas?

"Why? Because he abandoned my sister and me. He never even tried to reach out to us...and now after all this time he wants to spend Christmas with us?"

"That's where you're wrong. He did try to reach out to you and your sister, but your mother wouldn't let him."

"Don't you dare speak bad about my mother like that. She wouldn't have dared keep us from him if he had been half a man and tried to see us!" he said. "He never reached out to us. And now it's too late."

"That's not what he told me, sir. He told me that he sent cards and letters and that your mother sent them all back," I explained. "I know Big Tony, and he wouldn't just abandon you like that. He's been like a father to me, especially since I don't know my father. If somebody called me and told me that my father was around and wanted to see me, I would jump at the chance."

"He dropped the ball."

"Everybody makes mistakes, sir."

"Look, son, you sound like a nice young man and it's nothing personal, but this conversation is over. Don't bother calling back here again. Tell my old man to pretend that I'm dead," he said, and before I could respond he'd hung up.

I sat at the kitchen table. Discouraged.

"What's the matter, Tee?" Arlene asked as she walked into the kitchen, grabbed a package of chicken from the freezer and placed it on the countertop to thaw.

"Nothing."

"You looking for Big Tony's kids again?" she asked, zeroing in on the phone book in front of me.

"I found his son."

"Really? You talked to him?"

I nodded yes, still discouraged by our conversation. I really didn't want to talk about it. I wanted to just let it all sink in.

"What happened?" Arlene asked. "The look on your face tells me that it didn't go well."

"He pretty much said to tell Big Tony to pretend he was dead," I told her.

"Well, baby, you tried. That's the best you could do, now let it go," Arlene advised and rubbed the top of my head. "I thought it was really nice that Jade's family invited us to spend Christmas with them," she said to change the subject.

"Yeah, that was cool," I told her. "But I kinda met someone new…this girl that goes to Clark Atlanta University, and I really like her. I was hoping to see her on Christmas Day."

"A college girl, Tee?"

"She's so cool. Easy to talk to. And we have so much in common."

"What about Jade?"

"She didn't even have my back when I needed her the most," I explained, reliving the day that Jade walked out of my life. She walked back in, but by then my feelings were different, and I didn't know how to tell her.

"You can't string her along then, Tee. You have to tell her that you're not feeling the same," Arlene said. "It's okay to date other people. You're still young. But you have to be a man and be up-front with these girls."

"I will, Arlene."

She took a seat at the kitchen table. Shut the white pages and pushed them aside.

"Got something I wanna talk to you about," she began. "I don't want you to call me Arlene anymore. I want you to call me Mama."

That alarmed me. We had called her Arlene for as long as I could remember, and anytime we slipped up and called her Mama in the past, she was quick to correct us. Sometimes we were close to being whipped if we forgot too many times.

"Where did that come from?" I asked.

"I know I haven't been much of a mother to you, Trey and Syd, but I'm trying. I wanna feel like a mama, and a good place to start is for you to call me Mama," she explained and smiled. "Is that okay with you?"

"That's cool with me, Mama," I said and smiled.

She was changing, and I could tell. And for the best. If it was possible for a child to be proud of his mother, then I was there. There were nights when we'd spent the entire night talking, even though I had to go to school the next day. It didn't matter to me. She needed me, and I wanted to be there for her. Later she told me that I had saved her from making a bad decision. Had I not talked her through the night, she would've given up and headed for the streets again. She was much stronger now.

"We can spend Christmas with Jade's family if you want to," I told her. "I still want to be her friend."

"It's up to you, baby," she answered and stood. She poured herself a glass of sweet tea and before leaving the kitchen said, "You just let me know what you want to do."

I sat there with a million thoughts rushing through my head. If we were spending the day with Jade's family, some decisions needed to be made. Christmas presents needed to be bought. Couldn't go empty-handed, I thought as I tried to remember what Jade said she wanted for Christmas. I decided on a bracelet I'd seen at the mall a couple of weeks ago. I would have her initials engraved on the back. And for Jennifer, I'd seen the nicest silver tennis bracelet, even though she told me not to buy her anything.

I called her two days after she'd scribbled her phone number into the palm of my hand and from that moment it was on. The first night we talked for three whole hours, the second night we talked for four. And the difference in our ages never seemed to matter. She had me thinking of her every minute of the day, wondering if she was thinking of me, too. I kept telling myself that we could never work, that Jade was a more realistic choice, but then I would hear Jennifer's sweet voice on the other end of my phone and everything would change.

She was spending Christmas with her father and sisters in Savannah and was leaving on Christmas morning. So I decided to arrange that we exchange gifts on Christmas Eve, and then I'd spend Christmas Day with Jade. They were the perfect plans. Jade had already sent me a text message with her future stepmother's address, and I had scribbled it inside my geometry notebook. I'd asked if I could invite Big Tony for Christmas and it was okay with her parents. When I invited him, he pretended that he had other plans that day, that his schedule was already booked. But after telling him that I really wanted him to come, he finally gave in.

"I'll come by for a little while, Youngblood," he'd said. "But I can't stay long."

I was sure he didn't have anything else to do that day, and I was excited that he'd agreed to come. Now the hard part—calling Anthony Jr. back and giving him the address, despite the fact that he'd told me not to call back. Just in case he changed his mind, I wanted him to have the address.

The phone rang three times before the answering machine picked up.

"Hello, Mr. Miller. This is Terrence Hill again. I talked to you earlier about your father. I know you said that you weren't interested in seeing him, but just in case you change your mind, I want to leave the address of where your father will be on Christmas Day. If you want to see him, you can come by 1125 Cypress Spring Road, in Powder Springs," I informed him and held on to the phone, wondering if I'd said everything that needed to be said. "Well, I guess that's all I wanted. If you need to reach me, my phone number should be on your caller ID. Hopefully you have caller ID. And hopefully I will see you on

Christmas. I would love to meet you. If not, happy holidays to you and your family. Thank you. Bye."

That was it. The deed was done.

twenty-eight

Jade

AS Nat King Cole's voice serenaded everyone in Veronica's family room, I helped her pull the turkey out of the oven, and pop the green-bean casserole in. Indigo cut up carrots and bell peppers for the tossed salad, while Tameka sliced the tomatoes. Mommy made gravy to go on top of her corn-bread dressing, and Nana Summer, Indigo's grandmother, gave everybody orders.

"We'll let this turkey sit here for a while before we slice it," Nana said. "In the meantime, Veronica, why don't you stir that pot of greens."

It was Veronica's first time meeting Nana Summer, but she instantly fell in love with her. And Nana Summer liked Veronica, too. That made me feel good. Nana had been like my grandmother, too, especially since I'd known Indigo since I was in elementary school, and Nana and I had history. Nana had a way with people, she always saw the good in them, and could tell right away if they weren't on the up-and-up. The fact that she liked Veronica said a lot. Mommy also seemed okay with her ex-husband's new fiancée. They were chitchatting like old friends, and helping each other in the kitchen like they'd known each other all their lives.

Veronica refreshed the hors d'oeuvres tray and sent me into the family room to take them to our guests. When I walked in there, Daddy and Indi's father, Mr. Summer, were singing along with Nat King Cole. Neither of them could sing, but they sure thought so as they held on to glasses filled with Jack Daniel's. Aunt Carolyn and Mel sat in the corner of the room, talking about whatever mothers talked about—their kids, discounts they had received at the neighborhood stores, or recipes they had tried that either worked or didn't work. They sipped on glasses filled with white wine and giggled about whatever it was they talked about. As I set the plate of hors d'oeuvres on the coffee table, the doorbell rang.

"Can you get that, Jade?" Veronica asked.

I peeked through the small curtain on the door, and Chocolate Boy's smile lit up the front porch. I returned the smile and swung the door opened. He greeted me with a hug and smelled like cologne. His mother hugged me, too.

"Hello, Jade," she said. "Good to see you again."

"Good to see you, too, Miss Hill," I said and smiled.

"I brought homemade rolls," Miss Hill admitted and

smiled, as she held a tray covered in aluminum foil. "Where's the kitchen?"

"That way," I said and pointed her in the direction of the kitchen.

"Hi, Jade," Sydney said and grabbed my hand and held it.

"Hey, Syd. You been good?"

"Yes. And Santa Claus came to my house," she announced.

"He did?" I asked as if I was surprised. "What did he bring you?"

"He brought me two Barbies, a new backpack, a Scrabble game, two new outfits, Sudoku books and some other stuff."

"Wow, you must've been really good this year," I said. "What about you, Trey?"

"I got a new dirt bike, and some Playstation games."

"Come on inside. I want to introduce you all to everybody."

I led the way to the family room first, introduced Terrence and his brother and sister to everyone in there. Then I led them to the kitchen. Terrence's mom had already introduced herself to Nana Summer, my mother and Veronica.

"He's cute," Veronica whispered into my ear and I couldn't help but smile. "Jade, why don't you get your guests something to drink?"

I did as she asked, and ended up pouring every one of

them a glass of sweet tea. Miss Hill jumped right in and started helping in the kitchen. Sydney and Trey rushed off to the upstairs with Mattie, where she introduced them to her new Playstation game that she had gotten for Christmas. Terrence and I snuck away into the formal living room.

"So was it hard to find the house?" I asked and plopped down onto the love seat and hoped that he would sit right next to me, but instead he sat in the chair across from me.

"No, we came right to it," he told her and reached into the pocket of his jacket. "Got something for you."

Chocolate Boy handed me a little white box with a gold bow on top. My heart pounded at the thought that I might find a promise ring inside. I hoped anyway, as I lifted the top off the box. It was a beautiful silver bracelet, and I held it into the air. On the back, my initials were engraved—JM. It was pretty, but definitely not a promise ring. I tried not to look disappointed, but it was hard. Instead I hugged his neck tightly and said, "Thank you."

"You're welcome," he said and grinned. "I saw that for you weeks ago, and I've been saving up so that I could buy it for you."

"I like it," I said and looked under the Christmas tree for his gift. I found it underneath some other stuff and handed it to him. "I got you something, too."

He opened the box and held in his hands the new Jordan tennis shoes. They were expensive, and I had been saving my allowance since October. My allowance was only able to cover half the cost, and where I fell short, Veronica covered the difference. I had to enlist Marcus's private-eye skills in order to get his shoe size, but I did it.

"You bought me Jordans?" he asked. "These are tight, Morgan. Thank you."

Did he say *Morgan?* It had been weeks since he called me by the nickname that only he had given me. Lately he'd been calling me Jade, and the first time he did it, I knew something was wrong. It was nice to be called Morgan again.

"You're welcome."

Our moment was interrupted by the doorbell and I wondered how many more people would gather at Veronica's house. When Veronica escorted a tall man into the formal living room, I wasn't sure who he was. He wore an afro—a style that I thought had played out before my mommy and daddy's time. He was a big man, with a big stomach and I couldn't place him.

"Big Tony." Terrence stood and gave him a handshake.

"Hey there, Youngblood," Big Tony said. "Merry Christmas."

"Same to you. I'm glad you could make it," Terrence said. "I want you to meet Jade. Jade, this is Big Tony that I talk about all the time."

"So this is the young lady you took to the dance?" he asked. "She's pretty."

"Hi," I said softly. "I've heard a lot about you, Big Tony."

"I've heard a lot about you, too. And you're much

prettier than Terrence described." His hand nearly swallowed mine. "Very nice to meet you, Jade."

"You, too," I said. "Can I get you something to drink?"

"Oh, no. I saw some folks that I know in there...Rufus Carter...I been doing repairs on his car for years, and Henry Summer..." It appeared he was already acquainted. "They already offered me something to drink, and I think I'll take them up on it."

When he mentioned Mr. Carter's name, I wondered how long they'd been there and if Marcus was there, too. He and Indigo had probably snuck away to the game room upstairs for a round on the video games or into the sunroom at the back of the house for a private moment.

"Just relax and make yourself at home," Chocolate Boy told Big Tony as if it was his home.

It was easy to do—think of Veronica's house as your own home, because it was so cozy. It felt like home to everyone who was there that day. You could see it on their faces and hear it in their voices as some of them sang along to James Brown's "Santa Claus Goes Straight to the Ghetto."

I was grateful for the privacy again, as Big Tony went into the family room with the rest of the men. I needed to be alone with Terrence just a little while longer. Needed to see if my Christmas wish would come true. I wondered if he still cared for me the way he did before, and if we had a future together. I wanted the answer to be yes, he cared about me the same or even more, and that we had a future together. I was prepared for the worst, and would take Veronica's advice and date other people if Terrence was ready to move on. I would be hurt, but it wouldn't be the end of the world.

"Are we still going out together, Terrence, because I haven't been sure in a while," I blurted and just put it out there.

He hesitated for a moment, and hesitation was never a good thing when talking about things like this.

"I like you a lot, Jade," he said.

"But?"

"No buts," he said.

That's it? He likes me a lot.

"Do we have a future together or not, Terrence?"

"I think we should take things one day at a time," he said. "See where life takes us."

That really wasn't the answer I was looking for. And when Veronica called everyone to the table for dinner, I knew that it was the only answer I was getting for the moment. I didn't exactly get my Christmas wish, but my dreams weren't shattered either.

twenty-nine

Terrence

christmas was never the right day to break people's hearts. You can do it on the Fourth of July or Labor Day, but never on Christmas Day. I couldn't bring myself to tell Jade what I was really thinking—that we should take a break for now…that I had met someone new and was crazy about her…that I cared about her, and wanted us to remain as friends. I couldn't do it. Not on Christmas Day.

As we all stood around the dinner table and Indigo's Nana Summer prayed over the food, I prayed for the right words to say to Jade Morgan. Just as Jade wondered about her future with me, I wondered about my future with Jennifer. Wondered if she could live with a boy who was much younger and still in high school. Or if she was only interested in friendship, when I wanted so much more.

I'd borrowed my mother's car the night before, rushed over to her dorm to surprise her. When I told her that I was outside, she came out wearing a sweatshirt with the words *AU CENTER* plastered across the front of it, a pair of skin-tight jeans and her hair was pulled back into a ponytail.

"Hey, Terrence, what you up to?" she asked.

"I knew you were leaving for Savannah in the morning. Wanted to bring you a Christmas gift," I explained and handed the small white box to her. "Merry Christmas."

"I didn't get you anything," she confessed and poked her lip out and then smiled as she opened the box. "Oh, how cute!"

"I was hoping you liked it."

"I love it."

Her arms wrapped tightly around my neck as she pressed her pelvis against me. I couldn't help but touch her lips with mine and before I knew it, my tongue was probing the inside of her mouth. My arms squeezed her little waist as I pulled her closer. She didn't pull away, she moved in closer. And I forgot all about the fact that the brisk night air was slapping against my face with a vengeance.

"Merry Christmas, Terrence," she whispered.

"I want you to be my girl...exclusively..." I suggested and felt as if I was stumbling over my words, but I stayed strong.

"Really?" she asked, surprised.

"Yes, really. I want you all to myself," I said.

"Why don't we talk about it when I get back from Savannah?" she asked. "Will that be cool?"

"Um...yeah...okay," I said. "We'll talk about it then."

"Well, I gotta go, Terrence. Gotta finish packing and getting myself together for my trip in the morning. I've decided to spend my Christmas break with my family. So I guess I'll see you in a couple weeks, okay?"

"Can I call you?"

"Of course you can. I'll have my cell phone," she informed me and smiled. "Let's keep in touch over the holidays."

She left me wondering what the answer to my question would be when she returned.

After Nana Summer had blessed the food, we all piled our plates with turkey and dressing, greens, macaroni and cheese and lots of other good things to eat. The echoes from forks hitting plates were just about all you could hear throughout the house. Jade pulled up a chair next to mine in the kitchen and we sat at the same table with Marcus, Indigo and Tameka. We laughed and talked about school and teachers we didn't like. The conversation was light and I was able to steer clear of the heavy conversation that Jade and I had earlier. I just wanted to enjoy the festivities of Christmas.

Just as I took a bite of my New York–style cheesecake, the doorbell rang.

"Oops, somebody missed dinner," Marcus said.

"Too bad, because that was one of the best meals I ever had," Tameka chimed in.

My stomach was so full, I could barely move, but I managed to pour myself another glass of tea.

"I can't believe Miss Ryan gave us homework over the Christmas holidays," Indigo complained.

"She's stupid," Jade added. "I haven't even touched mine yet."

"Me, either," Indigo confessed and stuffed cheesecake into her mouth. "I think some teachers who are lonely and don't have a life purposely try to make yours miserable."

"If she had a husband and family, she wouldn't give us homework over the Christmas holidays. That's just plain stupid."

Arlene stuck her head into the kitchen, and I wondered if Sydney or Trey needed something.

"Baby, I think you should come in here for a second. There's something you need to see."

As I followed her to the family room, Jade, Indigo and Marcus were right behind me. Big Tony stood in the center of the room embracing a man who looked like him—with the same shaped head. They were just about the same height and build, and their faces were almost identical.

"That's Big Tony's son," Arlene whispered. "His daughter is over there on the couch. And these are all of his little grandchildren."

When Big Tony looked my way, I could've sworn I saw tears in his eyes.

"Terrence," he called when he spotted me. "Come on in here and meet my family."

"Oh, this is the young man who called me," Big Tony's son said and extended his hand. "I'm Anthony."

"Nice to meet you," I replied and shook his hand. "I'm Terrence."

"And this here's my daughter, Adrienne." Big Tony's daughter stood and instead of taking my hand, she pulled me into her, hugged me tightly.

Tears filled her eyes as she softly said, "Thank you for doing this."

"So you set all this up, Youngblood?" Big Tony asked.

"I wanted you to know what it was like to spend Christmas with family, instead of spending it with your head underneath the hood of some car. And I knew how bad you wanted a relationship with your kids. I wanted them to know the truth about you…that you didn't abandon them…"

"Yeah, I called my mother the minute I got off the phone with you," Anthony explained. "Forced her to tell me the truth. I couldn't believe she had kept us away from our father like that. We missed so much time with him."

"And we have children who had never met their grandfather," Adrienne said. "But thanks to Terrence, we can begin to change that."

"We are so sorry that we are just now doing this," Anthony told his father. "But from now on things will be different."

Big Tony's whole face was wet and before I knew it, Jade was handing him a handful of tissues. He always had a tough exterior, and this was the first time I'd ever seen him so broken. It caused my own eyes to run a little, and when I looked around, there wasn't a dry eye in the house.

Everyone had gathered to see what all the commotion was in the family room. As Big Tony lifted his grandson into the air and twirled him around, I knew that this would be his last Christmas alone. And I was happy for him.

Arlene wrapped her arm around my waist. "You did a good thing, son," she whispered. "A very good thing."

"I'm just glad it worked out."

"Me, too," she said. "Because it could've backfired in your face, but God has a way of bringing things together when they're supposed to be together."

"Yeah, he brought you back home to your family, too," I whispered.

"Yes, he did," she said. "With your help."

As I kissed Arlene's forehead and looked over at Big Tony and his family, I knew that Christmas would never be the same for me or him. It was forever changed.

thirty

Jade

Long after dance team practice was over, I stood in the middle of the buffed floors, the music playing in my head as I moved to it. It was Mary J. Blige singing her old-school tune "No More Drama." I created my own rhythm and my body was like poetry in motion. I needed to remember why I wanted to be a dancer. Not just because I could dance, but because dancing was a part of me. It was my art. It was my reason.

I danced because it was the one thing that kept me focused. When I was sad, it cheered me up. When I was scared, it calmed my fears. It made me better. Miss Moore always taught us that if dancing was our passion then it would cause everything around us to change. For some reason, it wasn't able to change the aching that I felt in my heart at that moment. I knew that it would pass, and

I'd be okay, but for right now it hurt. Hurt almost as bad as my parents' divorce. It hurt more than the moment my daddy announced that he was marrying Veronica.

Being Chocolate Boy's friend would be hard, especially when I still had feelings for him. He was sweet and I had learned things from him, like how to be responsible and how not to judge others, so for him I would try. And just like Veronica said, sometimes people came into our lives for a moment to teach us things. And the time that we spent together had been time well spent, and I shouldn't regret one single moment.

Once the music stopped playing in my head, I took a seat on the bleachers just to catch my breath. Sat there for a moment, my arms resting on my knees, my eyes staring at my Nike tennis shoes. The tears in my eyes threatened to fall if I didn't do something fast. I cried. My heart had been broken before, but it never felt like this. This felt like I wouldn't recover, like it would never end.

My chest hurt, and I continued to cry.

This would've been easier if Chocolate Boy had treated me badly, but he didn't. Instead, he started off by telling me how beautiful I was, and that he had learned so much from me.

"Jade, I care about you a lot, but my heart is somewhere else," he had said. "I don't even know if this person wants to be with me like that, but all I know is I can't keep you hanging around like this. That would only hurt you more."

He had met someone new. That was all I heard. That

was the part that stung, the part that made my heart ache. I would miss Chocolate Boy, but there would be plenty of others with that same sparkle in their eyes. I just had to be patient.

"I knew just where to find you," Indigo said as she walked into the gymnasium and softly shut the door behind her. "Are you okay?"

"I'm okay," I said and tried to shake the tears before she got closer. Didn't want anyone to see me cry.

Indigo sat down beside me, took my hand in hers. She wiped tears from my eyes.

"This is only temporary. You know that, don't you? Remember when I caught Quincy at the movies with Patrice. I thought that I would die. It hurt so bad, Jade, I thought that dying would feel better. It passed though. And this, too, shall pass."

"I know," I admitted to my best friend. "What hurts is that I thought Terrence was different."

"He is different. And he's still a very sweet guy…maybe just not for you. There will be others, Jade, I promise."

Indigo stood, pulled me up from the bleachers.

"Let's go, girl."

With a new stepmother that I was beginning to like more and more each day, a best friend that was always there for me and a bright future, I couldn't go wrong. As Indigo and I left the gym, she wrapped her arm around my neck.

I began to sing the words to "No More Drama" aloud. Indigo caught on to what I was singing, and began to sing along.

"Why are we singing 'No More Drama'?" Indigo finally asked after we'd sung almost the whole song.

"Because I like it."

"You know...now that Terrence is out of the picture, there's a chance you might bump into Usher at the Wal-Mart."

"I know. And I might even give him a chance to holler at me."

"He probably would, too," Indigo added and laughed. "But only after he finished his shopping."

"Only after I finished my shopping! It's all about me now," I said. "I've decided that I'm definitely going to Spelman, Indi. I know you mentioned some school up north so you could be near Marcus. But I've made my choice. It's Spelman for me."

"That's good. It's probably the best choice, Jade. I'm proud of you for deciding."

"I've signed up to take the SAT next semester so that I can find out where my score is," I declared and smiled. "And guess what...I went and got fitted for my bridesmaid dress the other day."

"For real? So you've decided to be in the wedding?"

"How could I not? Veronica's like family now," I said. "I can't believe I just said that."

"I can't either, when just a couple of months ago you wanted to put a hit out on her."

"Things change, people change. Attitudes adjust, Indi."

"I think you're growing up, Jade."

"I know I am. A month ago, I would've been mad at Terrence for breaking my heart. But just like Mommy said, it's not what you go through, but how you go through it. It's all about how you handle things."

"Your mom's right," Indigo said as we approached the boys' gym where their practice had ended.

My phone buzzed and I pulled it out of my pocket in order to read the text message.

"What u doin?" Chocolate Boy asked.

"Just leavin da gym," I replied.

"Me 2. Can I walk you home?"

I thought about it for a moment. Being friends with Terrence might not be a bad thing. I looked up from my phone and he was staring at me from across the room.

"Well?" he asked.

"Yeah. You can walk me home," I said.

"You sure?"

"I'm sure," I said. "But there's a catch."

"What's that?"

"You gotta buy me an ice-cream cone from McDonald's."

"I can handle that, Morgan," he said. "Can you handle this…friendship?"

"I can handle anything, dude. I'm Jade Morgan."

He held the door open and I walked through it, right into the sunshine of a brand-new day.

I was a brand-new Jade—improved, untarnished, un-Jaded.